T0176214

GEORGES SIMENON

The Misty Harbour

Translated by LINDA COVERDALE

PENGUIN BOOKS

PENGUIN CLASSICS

UK | USA | Canada | Ireland | Australia
India | New Zealand | South Africa

Penguin Books is part of the Penguin Random House group of companies
whose addresses can be found at global.penguinrandomhouse.com.

Penguin
Random House
UK

First published in French as *Le port des brumes* by Fayard 1932
This translation first published in Penguin Books 2015

012

Copyright 1932 by Georges Simenon Limited
Translation copyright © Linda Coverdale, 2015
GEORGES SIMENON ® Simenon.tm
MAIGRET ® Georges Simenon Limited
All rights reserved

The moral rights of the author and translator have been asserted

Set in Dante MT Std 12.5/15pt
Typeset by Palimpsest Book Production Limited, Falkirk, Stirlingshire
Printed and bound in Great Britain by Clays Ltd, Elcograf S.p.A.

ISBN: 978-0-141-39479-4

Contents

PENGUIN CLASSICS

The Misty Harbour

'I love reading Simenon. He makes me think of Chekhov'
— William Faulkner

'A truly wonderful writer . . . marvellously readable – lucid, simple, absolutely in tune with the world he creates'
— Muriel Spark

'Few writers have ever conveyed with such a sure touch, the bleakness of human life'   — A. N. Wilson

'One of the greatest writers of the twentieth century . . . Simenon was unequalled at making us look inside, though the ability was masked by his brilliance at absorbing us obsessively in his stories'   — *Guardian*

'A novelist who entered his fictional world as if he were part of it'   — Peter Ackroyd

'The greatest of all, the most genuine novelist we have had in literature'   — André Gide

'Superb . . . The most addictive of writers . . . A unique teller of tales'   — *Observer*

'The mysteries of the human personality are revealed in all their disconcerting complexity'   — Anita Brookner

'A writer who, more than any other crime novelist, combined a high literary reputation with popular appeal' — P. D. James

'A supreme writer . . . Unforgettable vividness'
— *Independent*

'Compelling, remorseless, brilliant'   — John Gray

'Extraordinary masterpieces of the twentieth century'
— John Banville

Georges Simenon was born on 12 February 1903 in Liège, Belgium, and died in 1989 in Lausanne, Switzerland, where he had lived for the latter part of his life. Between 1931 and 1972 he published seventy-five novels and twenty-eight short stories featuring Inspector Maigret.

Simenon always resisted identifying himself with his famous literary character, but acknowledged that they shared an important characteristic:

> My motto, to the extent that I have one, has been noted often enough, and I've always conformed to it. It's the one I've given to old Maigret, who resembles me in certain points . . . 'understand and judge not'.

Penguin is publishing the entire series of Maigret novels.

1. The Cat in the House

When they had left Paris at around three o'clock, the streets were still bustling in the chilly late-autumn sunshine. Shortly afterwards, near Mantes, the lights had come on in the train compartment. Darkness had fallen outside by the time they reached Évreux, and now, through windows streaming with droplets, they saw a thick mist gleaming in soft haloes around the track lights.

Snug in his corner, resting his head against the back of the banquette, Detective Chief Inspector Maigret had not taken his half-closed eyes from the unlikely couple across from him.

Captain Joris was asleep. His clothes were wrinkled, his wig askew on his gleaming pate.

And Julie, clutching her imitation crocodile handbag, stared off into space while endeavouring, despite her fatigue, to look thoughtful.

Joris! Julie!

Inspector Maigret of the Police Judiciaire was used to having people suddenly take over his life like this, monopolize him for days, weeks, months, and then sink back into the anonymous crowd.

The rhythmic sound of the wheels carried his thoughts along, and they were always the same at the beginning of each case: would this investigation be challenging or dull? Thankless and demoralizing, or painfully tragic?

As Maigret considered Joris, a faint smile touched his lips. A strange fellow! And for five days back at Quai des Orfèvres, everyone had called him That Man, because they couldn't find out who he was.

A man picked up for wandering in obvious distress among the cars and buses on the Grands Boulevards. Questioned in French, he remains mute. They try seven or eight languages. Nothing. Sign language proves fruitless as well.

A madman? In Maigret's office, he is searched. His suit is new, his underwear is new, his shoes are new. All identifying labels have been removed. No identification papers. No wallet. Five crisp thousand-franc bills have been slipped into one of his pockets.

The inquiry could not be more aggravating! Criminal records and case files are searched. Telegrams are sent at home and abroad. And although subjected to exhausting interrogation, That Man smiles affably all day long! A stocky fellow of about fifty, broad-shouldered, who neither protests nor gets upset, who smiles and sometimes seems to try to remember, but gives up almost immediately . . .

Amnesia? When the wig slides off his head they discover that a bullet has pierced his skull not more than two months earlier. The doctors marvel: whoever operated on him displayed superb surgical skill.

Fresh telegrams go out to hospitals and nursing homes in France, Belgium, Germany, Holland . . .

Five whole days of these painstaking investigations. The absurd results obtained by analysing some stains on his clothing and fine debris from his pockets: traces of salted cod's roe, dried and pulverized on the far shores of Norway for sardine bait.

Does That Man come from up there? Is he Scandinavian? There are indications that he has travelled a long way by train. But how can he have done this on his own, without speaking, with the befuddled appearance that makes him so conspicuous?

His picture appears in the newspapers. A telegram arrives from Ouistreham: *Unknown man identified!*

The telegram is followed by a woman – more of a girl, really – who shows up in Maigret's office, her haggard face inexpertly rouged and powdered: Julie Legrand, the mystery man's maid.

He is no longer That Man: he has a name and a profession. He is Yves Joris, formerly a captain in the merchant navy, now the harbourmaster at Ouistreham, a small port between Trouville and Cherbourg in Lower Normandy.

Julie bursts into tears! Julie cannot understand! Julie begs him to speak to her! And he looks at her calmly, pleasantly, the way he looks at everyone.

Captain Joris had disappeared from Ouistreham on 16 September. It is now the end of October.

What has happened to him while he was missing for six weeks?

'He went out to the lock to work the tide, as usual. An evening tide. I went off to bed. The next morning, he wasn't in his room . . .'

On account of the fog that night, everyone thinks Joris had slipped and fallen into the water. They hunted for him with grappling hooks. Then they assumed he had simply gone off for some peculiar reason of his own.

'Lisieux! . . . Departure in three minutes!'

Maigret goes to stretch his legs on the platform and refill his pipe. He has smoked so much since Paris that the air in the compartment has turned grey.

'All aboard!'

In the meantime Julie has powdered her nose; her eyes are still a bit red from weeping.

It's strange . . . There are moments when she is pretty, with a certain polish. At other times, though it would be hard to say why, she seems like a gauche little peasant.

She straightens the wig on the captain's head, for *her monsieur*, as she puts it, and looks at Maigret as if to say: 'Haven't I every right to take care of him?'

For Joris has no family. He has lived alone, for years, with Julie, whom he calls his housekeeper.

'He treated me like his daughter . . .'

As far as anyone knows, he has no enemies! Has had no adventures, no love affairs, no grand passions!

A man who, after sailing the seven seas for thirty years, could not resign himself to idleness and, despite his retirement, applied for the position of harbourmaster at Ouistreham. He had a small house built there . . .

And one fine evening, on 16 September, he vanished – then reappeared in Paris six weeks later in this sorry state.

Having never seen him in anything but a naval officer's

uniform, Julie had been dismayed to find him wearing an off-the-peg grey suit.

She is anxious, uneasy. Whenever she looks at the captain, her face reflects both pity and a nameless fear, a haunting anguish. It really is him, obviously! It's *her monsieur*, all right. And yet, he is no longer completely himself.

'He'll get well again, won't he? I'll take good care of him . . .'

The mist is now turning into large, blurry drops on the windows. Maigret's big, stolid face rocks a little from side to side as the train rattles along. Placidly, he goes on watching his companions: Julie, who pointed out to him that they might just as well have travelled third class, as she normally does, and Joris, who is waking up only to look around him vacantly. One more stop, at Caen. Then on to Ouistreham.

'Around a thousand people live in the village,' a colleague originally from there had told Maigret. 'The harbour is small but important, because of the canal linking the roadstead to the city of Caen. The canal can handle ships of five thousand tons or more.'

Maigret doesn't bother trying to imagine what the place looks like; he knows that's a fool's game. He waits, and his eyes keep turning to the wig, which hides the raw pink scar.

When Captain Joris disappeared, he had thick, dark brown hair with only a touch of silver at the temples. Another torment for Julie, who can't bear the sight of his bare skull . . . Every time the wig slips, she quickly straightens it.

'In short, someone tried to kill him . . .'

He was shot, and that's a fact. But he was also given the very best of medical care. He had no money when he vanished – yet was found with five thousand francs in his pocket.

But there is more to come. Julie suddenly opens her handbag.

'I forgot! I brought along the captain's mail.'

Almost nothing. Brochures for marine supplies. A receipt for dues paid to the Association of Merchant Navy Captains. Postcards from friends still in the service, including one sent from Punta Arenas . . .

A letter from the Banque de Normandie, in Caen. A printed form, the blanks filled in on a typewriter.

> . . . beg to inform you that the sum of three hundred thousand francs has been transferred as per your instructions from the Dutch Bank in Hamburg and credited to your Account No. 14173 . . .

And Julie has already insisted over and over that the captain is not a wealthy man! Maigret looks from one to the other of the pair seated across from him.

Salted cod's roe . . . Hamburg . . . The made-in-Germany shoes . . . And only Joris could explain all this. Joris, who beams a nice broad smile his way because he sees that Maigret is looking at him . . .

'This station is Caen! Passengers for Cherbourg remain on board; change here for Ouistreham, Lion-sur-Mer, Luc . . .'

It is seven o'clock. The air is so humid that the lights on the platform can barely shine through the milky mist.

'How do we go on to our destination now?' Maigret asks Julie as the other passengers push past them.

'Well, the local train runs only twice a day in the winter . . .'

There are taxis outside the station. Maigret is hungry. Having no idea what awaits him in Ouistreham, he prefers to have dinner in the station buffet.

Captain Joris is still behaving well and eats what he is served, like a child who trusts those in charge of him. A passing railway employee pauses at their table to consider the captain.

'Isn't that the harbourmaster of Ouistreham?' he asks Maigret, and twirls a finger at his temple. At a nod from Maigret he goes on his way, visibly amazed.

As for Julie, she takes refuge in practical matters.

'Twelve francs for a dinner like this, and it wasn't even cooked with butter! As if we couldn't simply have eaten when we got home . . .'

As she speaks, Maigret is thinking, 'A bullet in the head . . . Three hundred thousand francs . . .'

He stares searchingly into the captain's innocent eyes, while his mouth sets in a hard line.

The next taxi in line, once a fine limousine, has lumpy seats and creaking joints. The three passengers must crowd together in the back because the jump seats are broken, and Julie is pinned between the two men, squashed by first one, then the other, as the car swerves.

'I'm trying to remember if I locked the garden gate!'

she murmurs, increasingly concerned about her domestic duties as they get closer to the house.

Leaving the village, they literally drive into a wall of fog. A horse and cart appear abruptly, barely two metres away, like phantoms, and the trees and houses flitting by on both sides of the road seem like ghosts as well.

The driver slows down. They're going barely ten kilometres an hour, which doesn't prevent a man on a bicycle from bursting out of the fog and into the side of the taxi, which stops. The cyclist is unhurt.

As they go through Ouistreham, Julie rolls down the partition window to speak to the driver.

'Keep going to the harbour and across the swing bridge . . . Then stop at the cottage that's right by the lighthouse!'

Between the village and the harbour lies about a kilometre of road, now deserted, outlined by the feeble glow of streetlamps. At one corner of the bridge they see a lighted window and hear voices.

'That tavern is the Buvette de la Marine,' Julie points out. 'Everyone in the harbour spends most of their time in there.'

Beyond the bridge there's hardly any road at all, and what little there is goes wandering through the marshes along the banks of the Orne, leading at last only to the lighthouse and a cottage surrounded by a garden.

When they stop, Maigret watches the captain, who gets out of the taxi as calmly as you please and walks over to the gate.

'Did you see that, inspector!' cries Julie delightedly.

'He recognizes the house! I'm sure he'll eventually be completely himself again.'

She fits the key into the lock, pushes open the squeaky gate and heads up the gravel path. After paying the driver, Maigret quickly joins her, but now that the taxi is gone it is pitch dark.

'Would you mind striking a match? I can't find the keyhole . . .'

A tiny flame; the door is opened. A dark form brushes past Maigret's legs. Already inside, Julie switches on the light and, looking curiously along the floor, asks softly, 'That was the cat going outside just now, wasn't it?'

She takes off her hat and coat with practised ease, hangs them on a coat peg, pushes open the door to the kitchen and turns on the light, thus inadvertently revealing that this is the room where everyone usually gathers.

A well-lit kitchen with tiled walls, a big sand-scoured pine table, sparkling copper pots and pans. And the captain goes automatically to sit in his wicker armchair over by the stove.

'But I'm sure I put the cat out when I left, the way I always do . . .'

She's worried, talking to herself.

'Yes, I'm certain of it. I left all the doors locked. Oh, inspector, would you please go through the house with me? I'm frightened . . .'

So much so that she hardly dares to go first. She opens the door to the dining room, where all is in such perfect order, with the furniture and parquet polished to a fare-thee-well, that it's clear the room is never used.

9

'Look behind the curtains, would you?'

There are pieces of Chinese lacquerware and porcelain the captain must have brought back from the Far East, and an upright piano.

Then the living room, just as tidy, with the furniture as spotless as on the day it was bought. The captain is tagging along, pleased, almost blissful. They go upstairs, walking on a red carpet runner. There are three bedrooms, one of which is a spare.

And everywhere, that same cleanliness, that meticulous order, that faint smell of cooking and countryside.

No one is hiding there. The windows are shut and bolted. The garden gate is locked, although the key has been left outside.

'Perhaps the cat came in through a basement window,' Maigret tells her.

'There are none.'

They return to the kitchen; she opens a cupboard.

'May I offer you a drop of something?'

And it is now, amid these ritual movements, while pouring a liqueur into tiny glasses decorated with painted flowers, that she feels her anguish most deeply and begins to sob.

She looks furtively at the captain, who is back in his armchair. The sight of him is so painful that she looks away and, stammering with the effort to pull herself together, tells Maigret, 'I'll make the guest room ready for you.'

She can hardly get the words out. She takes an apron hanging on the wall to wipe her eyes.

'I would rather stay at the hotel. I suppose there is one . . .'

Julie looks up at a small china clock, the kind often won at a fairground, a clock that ticks along like the comforting soul of the household.

'Yes! You'll still find someone there at this hour. It's on the other side of the lock, just behind the Buvette de la Marine.'

She wishes he would stay, however, and seems afraid to be left alone with the captain, whom she no longer dares look at.

'You don't think there's anyone in the house?'

'As you saw for yourself.'

'You'll come back tomorrow morning?'

She goes with him to the front door, which she shuts firmly behind him.

And Maigret finds himself plunging into fog so dense that he cannot even see his feet. He does manage to find the gate. He can feel that he is walking on grass, then on the rough, stony road. He also becomes aware of a distant noise that he will need some time to identify.

It resembles the lowing of a cow, but sadder, more desolate.

'Idiot!' he finally growls between his teeth. 'It's only the foghorn . . .'

He's no longer sure where he is. And now, right in front of his feet, he looks down at water that appears to be steaming. He is on the wall of the lock! He hears the screech of cranks turning somewhere. He can't remember where the taxi crossed the water and, spotting a narrow footbridge, he is about to step on to it.

'Watch out!'

He is stunned: the voice is so close to him! Just when Maigret was feeling absolutely alone, a man has turned up within three metres of him – and the inspector must strain to make out even his silhouette.

Now he understands that warning: the footbridge he was about to cross is moving. It's the gate of the lock itself that is opening, and the sight becomes even more hallucinatory because quite close by, a few metres away, it's no longer a man that appears but an entire wall, as high as a house. On top of this wall are lights shining fitfully through the mist.

A ship is passing – and Maigret could reach out to touch it! When the end of a hawser thuds down near him, someone picks it up, lugs it to a bollard and makes it fast.

'Slow astern! . . . Stand by!' shouts someone up on the bridge of the steamer.

A few moments earlier, the place had seemed dead, deserted. And now Maigret, walking the length of the lock, sees that the mist is full of human figures. Someone is turning a winch. Another man runs up with a second mooring line. Customs officials are waiting for the gangway to be lowered to allow them aboard. And none of them can see a thing, in the thick mist that pearls in droplets on the men's moustaches.

'You want to cross over?'

The voice is quite close. Another lock-gate.

'Hurry up, or you'll have to wait a good fifteen minutes . . .'

He goes across holding on to the handrail, hears water boiling beneath his feet and, still in the distance, the moaning of the foghorn. The more Maigret advances, the more this world of mist fills with teeming, mysterious life. A light draws him on; approaching, he sees a fisherman, in a boat moored to the dock, lowering and raising a net attached to some poles.

The man glances at him without interest, then begins to sort through a basket of small fish.

The lights illuminating the mist around the ship make it easier to see what is going on. Up on deck, they're speaking English; a man in an officer's cap is initialling documents at the edge of the quay.

The harbourmaster! The replacement for Captain Joris . . .

Like Joris, the man is short, but he's thinner, more lively, and jokes around with the ship's officers.

The world has dwindled to a few square metres of patchy illumination and a vast black hole where water and terra firma make their invisible presence felt. The sea is over there, to the left, barely murmuring at all.

Wasn't it on a night like this that Joris suddenly vanished from the scene? He was checking papers, like his colleague now, and probably cracking jokes, too. He was keeping track of the sluicing water and all the activity. He had no need to see everything; a few familiar sounds would have been enough. Look at the way no one here watches where he's going!

Maigret has just lit a pipe and begins to scowl; he does not like to feel clumsy. He's angry with himself for being a ponderous landlubber for whom the sea is a source of fear or wonder.

The lock-gates open. The ship enters a canal almost as wide as the Seine in Paris.

'Forgive the interruption: are you the harbour-master? . . . Detective Chief Inspector Maigret, of the Police Judiciaire. I've just brought home your colleague.'

'Joris is here? So it really is he? . . . I heard about it this morning . . . But, is it true he's . . .'

And he gently taps his forehead.

'For the moment, yes. Will you spend all night here?'

'Never more than five hours at a stretch. As long as the tide lasts, basically! There are five hours during each tide when the ships have enough water to enter the canal or set out to sea, and this window shifts every day. Tonight, we've just begun and we'll be busy here until three in the morning . . .'

A straightforward man, who treats Maigret as a colleague, a public servant like himself.

'Would you excuse me?'

Then the harbourmaster looks out towards the open water, where there is nothing to see, and remarks, 'A sailing ship from Boulogne has tied up at the jetty to wait her turn at the canal.'

'Do you always know what ships to expect?'

'Most of the time. Especially the steamers. They're generally on a regular schedule, bringing coal from England, heading back from Caen loaded with ore.'

'Will you join me in a drink?'

'I can't, not until the tide has ebbed. I have to stay here.'

And the harbourmaster shouts orders to invisible men, knowing exactly where they are.

'You are conducting an inquiry?' he asks.

Just then they hear footsteps, coming from the village. A man goes across one of the lock-gates and as he passes a light, it gleams on the barrel of a rifle.

'Who is that?'

'The mayor, off to hunt ducks. He has a blind down by the Orne. His assistant must already be there getting things ready for tonight.'

'You think I'll find the hotel still open?'

'The Hôtel de l'Univers? Yes, but you'd best hurry . . . The owner will soon finish playing cards and head off to bed. And once there, he stays there!'

'Until tomorrow, then.'

'Fine. I'm due back here at ten, for the morning tide.'

They shake hands, like two phantoms in the mist. And life goes on in the fog, where one may suddenly bump into an invisible man.

The experience does not feel sinister, really; it's something else: a vague uneasiness, a faint oppressive anxiety, the impression of an unknown world with its own life going on all around you. A world in which you are a stranger.

That darkness peopled by invisible beings . . . That sailing ship, for example, waiting nearby for its turn, although you would never even guess it was there.

About to pass the fisherman again, sitting motionless under his lantern, Maigret tries to think of something to say.

'They biting tonight?'

And the other man merely spits into the water as Maigret walks on, kicking himself for having said something so stupid.

The last thing he hears before entering the hotel is the slamming of the upstairs shutters over at Captain Joris' cottage.

Julie, who is frightened! The cat escaping when they entered the house . . .

'That foghorn going to wail all night?' grumbles Maigret impatiently, as the landlord comes to greet him.

'As long as there's fog about . . . You get used to it . . .'

Maigret slept fitfully, the way one does with indigestion or as a child tosses and turns the night before some great event. Twice the inspector got up to lean his face against the cold windowpanes and saw nothing but the empty road and revolving lighthouse beam, which seemed to keep stabbing at a cloudbank. The eternal foghorn sounded harsher, more aggressive.

The second time, he checked his watch: four o'clock, and fishermen with baskets on their backs were clattering off to the harbour in their clogs.

Almost immediately there was a frantic pounding on his door, which opened without waiting for his response and revealed the anguished face of the landlord.

Some time had passed, however: although the foghorn was still going strong, sunshine now gleamed at the windows.

'Hurry! The captain is dying . . .'

'What captain?'

'Captain Joris . . . Julie's just rushed to the harbour to send for both you and a doctor.'

Maigret, his hair unbrushed, was already pulling on his

trousers. He jammed his feet into his shoes without lacing them up and forgot to attach the stiff collar to his shirt before putting on his jacket.

'You'll have nothing before you go? A cup of coffee? A tot of rum?'

No – he hadn't time! It was sunny outdoors, but quite chilly. The road was still damp with dew.

Hurrying across the lock, Maigret caught a glimpse of the sea, but only a small strip of it, perfectly still and pale blue; the rest was hidden by a long fogbank hanging just offshore.

Someone called to him from the bridge.

'Are you the detective chief inspector from Paris? I'm with the local police. I'm glad you've come . . . Have you already heard?'

'Heard what?'

'They say it's awful! . . . Wait a minute . . . There's the doctor's car . . .'

Fishing boats in the outer harbour were rocking gently, casting red and green reflections across the water. Some sails were set, probably to dry, and showed their black identity numbers.

Two or three women waited out by the lighthouse, in front of the captain's cottage. The door was open.

The doctor's car passed Maigret and the policeman, who was sticking close to the inspector.

'They're talking about poison,' the officer continued. 'It seems he's turned a greenish colour . . .'

Maigret entered the cottage just when Julie was coming slowly downstairs in tears, her eyes swollen, her cheeks flushed. She had been shooed out of the bedroom so the doctor could examine the dying man.

Under a hastily donned coat, she still wore a long white nightgown and her feet were bare in their slippers.

'It's terrible, inspector! You can't imagine . . . Go up, quickly! Maybe . . .'

The doctor had been bending over his patient and was just straightening up when Maigret entered the bedroom. The inspector could see from his face that it was hopeless.

'Police . . .'

'Ah! Well, it's the end. Maybe two or three minutes more . . . Either I'm way off course, or it's strychnine.'

Joris seemed to be straining to breathe, so the doctor opened a window. And there again was that dreamlike tableau: the sun, the harbour, the boats and their unfurled sails, fishermen pouring brimming baskets of glittering fish into crates.

What a contrast: the dying man's face seemed yellower, or greener, an indescribable colour. A neutral tone incompatible with any ordinary conception of flesh. His limbs were writhing, jerking spasmodically, yet his face remained calm, in seeming repose, as he stared at the wall in front of him.

Holding one of his patient's wrists, the doctor was tracking the weakening pulse when Maigret saw a look come over his face that said, 'Watch closely! He's going now . . .'

Then something amazing and quite poignant happened. The captain's face had been so empty that no one could tell if the wretched man had recovered his reason, but now this face came back to life. As if he were a boy on the verge of tears, his features crumpled into a pitiful expression of misery so deep that it cannot go on.

And two great tears welled up, about to spill over . . .

Almost at the same instant, the doctor announced softly, 'It's over.'

Could that have happened? Could death have come at the very moment Joris was weeping?

And while those tears were still alive, trickling down to vanish within his ears, the captain himself was dead.

They heard footsteps in the stairwell. Surrounded by women, Julie was sobbing and gasping below. Maigret went out to the landing.

'No one,' he said slowly, 'is to enter this room!'

'Is he . . . ?'

'Yes!' he replied firmly.

And he went back to the sunny room, where the doctor, for his own peace of mind, was preparing to administer a heart injection.

Out on the garden wall, there was a pure white cat.

2. The Inheritance

Somewhere downstairs, probably in the kitchen, they could hear Julie's shrill cries as she struggled with her grief, restrained and surrounded by women from the neighbourhood.

The window was still wide open, and Maigret saw villagers arriving at a kind of half-run. Kids on bikes, women carrying babies, men in clogs – it was a disorganized and lively little procession that poured over the bridge and on towards the captain's house, just as if they had been drawn there by a travelling circus or a traffic accident.

Maigret soon had to close the window against the noise outside, and the muslin curtains softened the light. The atmosphere in the bedroom became milder, more subdued. The wallpaper was pink. The furniture of pale wood was well polished. A vase full of flowers held pride of place on the mantelpiece.

The inspector watched the doctor as he held up to the light a glass and a carafe of water he had taken from the bedside table. He even dipped a finger into the water and touched it to his tongue.

'That's what did it?'

'Yes. The captain must have liked to have a glass of water handy at night. As far as I can tell, he drank some at around three this morning, but I don't understand why he didn't call for help.'

'For the very good reason that he couldn't speak or even make the slightest sound,' muttered Maigret.

He summoned the policeman and told him to inform the mayor and the public prosecutor at Caen of what had happened. People were still coming and going downstairs, while outside, on that bit of road leading nowhere, the local folk were standing around in groups. A few, to be more comfortable, were sitting on the grass.

The tide was coming in, already invading the sandbanks by the entrance to the harbour. Smoke on the horizon betrayed a ship waiting for the right time to head in to the bay.

'Do you have any idea of . . .' the doctor began, but fell silent when he realized that the inspector was busy. Maigret had opened a mahogany writing desk that stood between the two bedroom windows and was making a list of what was in the drawers, with the obstinate frown he always wore on such occasions. Seen like that, the inspector looked somewhat brutish. He had lit his fat pipe, which he smoked in slow puffs, and his big fingers handled the things he was finding without any apparent care or respect.

Photographs, for example. There were dozens. Many were of friends, almost all of them in naval uniform and about the same age as Joris would have been at the time. Evidently he had kept in touch with his classmates at the marine academy in Brest, and they wrote to him from every corner of the world. Photos in postcard format, artless and banal, whether they arrived from Saigon or

Santiago: 'Hello from Henry,' or 'At last! My third stripe! Hooray! Eugène.'

Most of these cards were addressed to 'Captain Joris, aboard the *Diana*, Compagnie Anglo-Normande, Caen'.

'Had you known the captain long?' Maigret asked the doctor.

'For a good while. Ever since he came here. Before that, he sailed on one of the mayor's ships. Captained her for twenty-eight years.'

'The mayor's ships?'

'Yes, Monsieur Ernest Grandmaison! The chairman of the Compagnie Anglo-Normande. In effect, the sole owner of the company's eleven steamships.'

Another photograph: Joris himself this time, at twenty-five, already stocky, with a broad, smiling face, but a hint of stubbornness, too. A real Breton!

Finally, in a canvas folder, certificates, from his school diploma all the way to a master's certificate in the Merchant Navy, as well as official documents, his birth certificate, service record, passports . . .

Maigret picked up an envelope that had fallen to the floor. The paper was already yellowing with age.

'A will?' asked the doctor, who was at a loose end until the examining magistrate arrived.

The household of Captain Joris must have been run on trust, because the envelope was not even sealed. Within was a sheet of paper; the writing was in a neat, elegant hand.

I the undersigned Yves-Antoine Joris, born in Paimpol, a captain in the Merchant Navy, do hereby bequeath all my property, real and personal, to Julie Legrand, in my employ, in recompense for her years of devoted service.

I direct her to make the following bequests:

My canoe to Captain Delcourt; the Chinese porcelain dinner service to his wife; my carved ivory-headed cane to . . .

Almost everyone in that little harbour-town world, which Maigret had seen bustling in the fog the night before, had been remembered. Even the lock-keeper, who was to receive a fishing net, 'the trammel lying under the shed', as the captain had put it.

Just then there was a strange noise in the house. While the women in the kitchen were busy fixing Julie a hot toddy 'to buck her up', she had dashed upstairs and now entered the bedroom, looking wildly all around her. She then rushed towards the bed only to draw back, speechless before the spectacle of death.

'Is he . . . Can he be . . . ?'

She collapsed on to the carpet, wailing almost unintelligibly, but one could just make out: '. . . It can't be . . . My poor *monsieur* . . . my . . . my . . .'

Solemnly, Maigret stooped to help her to her feet and guide her, still shuddering in distress, into her bedroom next door. The place was in disorder, with clothes lying on the bed and soapy water in the wash basin.

'Who filled the water carafe sitting on the bedside table?'

'I did . . . Yesterday morning . . . When I put flowers in the captain's room . . .'

'Were you alone in the house?'

Julie was panting, slowly recovering her composure, yet beginning to wonder at the inspector's questions.

'What are you thinking?' she cried abruptly.

'I'm not thinking anything. Calm down. I've just read the captain's will.'

'And?'

'You inherit everything. You'll be rich . . .'

His words simply provoked fresh tears.

'The captain was poisoned by the water in the carafe.'

She glared at him with bristling contempt.

'What are you trying to say?' she shouted. 'What do you mean?'

She was so overwrought that she grabbed his forearm, shook it in fury and even seemed about to start hitting and clawing at him.

'Julie, compose yourself, listen to me! The inquiry has only just begun. I am not insinuating anything. I am gathering information.'

A loud knock at the door; the policeman had brought news.

'The magistrate cannot get here before early this afternoon. The mayor, who was out hunting last night, was in bed. He will come as soon as he's ready.'

Everyone was on edge. Throughout the house there was a fever of anxiety. And that crowd outside, waiting without really knowing what it was waiting for, increased the feeling of tension and disturbance.

'Are you planning on staying here?' Maigret asked Julie.

'Why not? Wherever would I go?'

The inspector asked the doctor to leave the captain's

bedroom, then locked the door behind him. He permitted only two women to remain with Julie, the wife of the lighthouse-keeper and a lock-worker's wife.

'Allow no one else in,' he told the policeman. 'If necessary, try to send these curiosity seekers away without making a fuss.'

The inspector himself left the cottage, made his way through the onlookers and walked to the bridge. The fog-horn was still sounding in the distance, but only faintly now, with the wind blowing offshore. The air was mild. The sun shone more brightly with each passing hour. The tide was rising.

Two lock workers were already arriving from the village to begin their shifts. On the bridge, Maigret saw Captain Delcourt, with whom he had spoken the previous evening and who now came towards him.

'Tell me! Is it true?'

'Joris was poisoned, yes.'

'Who did it?'

The people over at the cottage were beginning to disperse. The policeman seemed to be the reason, going from group to group, telling them God knows what and gesturing emphatically. Now, however, the crowd had fixed on the inspector and observed him intently.

'Are you already on duty?'

'Not yet. Not until the tide rises a good metre more. Look! That steamship you see at anchor in the roadstead has been waiting since six this morning.'

Customs officials, the head lock-keeper, the water bailiff and the skipper of the coastguard cutter were among the onlookers hovering nearby, not daring to approach the two men, but the lock workers were getting ready to start their shifts.

So Maigret was now seeing in broad daylight the men he had sensed had been working all around him the previous night, hidden in the fog. The Buvette de la Marine was only a few steps away, its windows and glass door providing a fine view of the lock, the bridge, the jetties, the lighthouse and Joris' cottage.

'Will you come and have a drink?' the inspector asked Captain Delcourt.

He had the feeling that this was customary, that with each tide this little fraternity would repair to their local hangout. The captain checked the level of the water.

'I've got half an hour,' he announced.

They both entered the simple wooden tavern, gradually followed – after some hesitation – by the others. Maigret beckoned to them to join him and his companion at their table.

He had to break the ice, introducing himself to everyone to inspire their trust and even gain some sort of access to their circle.

'What'll you have?'

They all glanced at one another, still a bit ill at ease.

'This time of day, it's usually coffee laced with a warming drop . . .'

A woman served them all. The crowd returning from the cottage tried to see inside the bar and, reluctant to go on home, scattered through the harbour to await developments.

After filling his pipe, Maigret passed his tobacco pouch around. Captain Delcourt preferred a cigarette, but the head lock-keeper, reddening slightly, tucked a pinch of tobacco inside his lip and mumbled, 'If you don't mind . . .'

Maigret finally made his move.

'A strange business, this, don't you think?'

They had all been expecting this moment, but the sally still met with an uncomfortable silence.

'Captain Joris seems to have been quite a fine fellow . . .'

And the inspector waited, darting discreet glances at the men's faces.

'Indeed!' replied Delcourt, who was a bit older than his predecessor, less tidy in his appearance and apparently not averse to drink.

Nevertheless, while speaking he kept a careful eye, through the curtains, on both the progress of the tide and the ship now weighing anchor.

'He's starting a mite early! The current in the Orne will shortly drive him on to the sandbanks . . .'

'Your health!' said Maigret. 'I take it, then, that none of you knows what happened on the night of the 16th of September . . .'

'No one. It was a foggy evening, like last night. I myself was not on duty. I stayed on here, though, playing cards with Joris and these other men here with you now.'

'Did you get together here every evening?'

'Just about . . . Not much else to do in Ouistreham. Three or four times, that night, Joris left his hand to someone else when he had to go and attend to a boat in the lock. By nine thirty, the tide had gone out. He set out into the fog, as if he were heading home.'

'When did you realize he was missing?'

'The next day. Julie came to ask about him. She'd gone to sleep before he got home and the next morning was astonished not to find him in his bedroom.'

'Joris had had a few drinks?'

'Never more than one!' insisted the customs man, growing eager to have his say on this subject. 'And no tobacco!'

'And . . . How shall I put this . . . He and Julie? . . .'

An exchange of looks, some hesitation, several smiles.

'No way to know. Joris swore there was nothing. It's just that . . .'

The customs man picked up the thread.

'I'm not speaking ill of him when I say that he didn't entirely fit in with the rest of us. He wasn't a prideful man, no, that's not the right word! But he paid attention to appearances, you understand? He'd never have come on duty in clogs, like Delcourt sometimes does. He played cards here of an evening, but never came by during the day. He never spoke familiarly to the lock workers . . . I don't know if you see what I'm getting at . . .'

Maigret saw perfectly. He had spent several hours in Joris' modest, cosy, neat little house. And now he considered the regulars at the Buvette de la Marine, a rowdier, more unbuttoned crew. This was a place for hearty drinking, where voices surely grew boisterous, the atmosphere thick with smoke, and the talk a touch coarse.

Joris came here simply to play cards, never chatted about his personal life, had only the one drink before leaving.

'She's been at his house for about eight years now. She was sixteen when she arrived, a little country girl, bedraggled and badly dressed . . .'

'And now . . .'

The waitress arrived as if on cue with a bottle of home-made brandy and poured another shot into the glasses, where only a little coffee remained. This, too, appeared to be the custom of the place.

'Now? She is what she is . . . At our dances, for example, she won't step out on the floor with just anyone. And in the shops, when she's treated with easy familiarity, like a maid, she gets angry. It's hard to explain . . . Even though her brother . . .'

The head lock-keeper gave the customs man a sharp look – but Maigret caught him at it.

'Her brother?'

'The inspector will find out anyway!' continued the man, who was obviously not on his first spiked coffee of the day. 'Her brother did eight years in prison. He was drunk, one night, in Honfleur. With a few others, loud and disorderly in the streets. When the police stepped in, the fellow hurt one officer so badly that he died the next month.'

'He's a sailor?'

'He served on ocean-going vessels in the foreign trade before coming back home. He's currently sailing on a schooner out of Paimpol, the *Saint-Michel*.'

Captain Delcourt had begun fidgeting nervously.

'Let's go!' he announced. 'It's time . . .'

'Before the steamer's even in the lock!' sighed the customs officer, clearly in less of a hurry.

Only three men were left. Maigret signalled to the waitress, who returned with her bottle.

'Does the *Saint-Michel* sometimes come through here?'

'Sometimes, yes.'

'Was she here on the 16th of September?'

'Well, it's going to be right there for him in the lock-keeper's log,' the customs man remarked to his neighbour and turned to Maigret: 'Yes, she was here. She even had to stay in the outer harbour on account of the fog and left only at daybreak.'

'Going where?'

'Southampton. I'm the one who looked over their papers. The cargo was grindstone grit, from Caen.'

'And Julie's brother hasn't been seen here since?'

This time the customs officer sniffed thoughtfully and paused before draining his glass.

'You'll have to ask those who claim to have spotted him yesterday . . . Me, I haven't seen a thing.'

'Yesterday?'

A shrug. An enormous steamer came gliding between the stone walls of the lock, a vast black mass towering over the countryside, its funnel taller than the trees lining the canal.

'I've got to get over there . . .'

'Me too . . .'

'How much does it come to, mademoiselle?' Maigret asked the waitress.

'The landlady isn't here just now, but I'm sure you'll be back.'

The people still waiting outside the captain's cottage for something to happen now gratefully turned their attention to the English steamer passing through the lock.

As Maigret left the bar, a man was arriving from the village; the inspector assumed he was the mayor, whom he had seen only briefly the night before.

A somewhat beefy fellow between forty-five and fifty, quite tall, with a rosy complexion. He was wearing a grey hunting coat and aviator gaiters. Maigret went over to him.

'Monsieur Grandmaison? I am Detective Chief Inspector Maigret of the Police Judiciaire.'

'Pleased to meet you,' came the casual reply.

The mayor looked at the Buvette de la Marine, then Maigret, then the tavern again as if to say, 'Strange company for an important official to keep!'

And he kept walking towards the lock on his way to the cottage.

'Joris is dead, I hear?'

'It's true,' replied Maigret, who did not much like the man's attitude.

An attitude that could hardly have been more traditional: that of the big fish in a small pond, someone who thinks himself the centre of the world, dresses like a country gentleman and pays a token tribute to democracy by shaking hands half-heartedly with his fellow citizens, saluting them with mumbled greetings and the occasional inquiry after their children's health.

'And you've caught the murderer? Since it was you who brought Joris here and who – excuse me . . .'

He went over to speak to the water bailiff, who apparently attended him when he went duck hunting.

'The left-hand reeds of the blind need straightening. And one of the decoys is useless, it looked half dead this morning.'

'I'll see to it, sir.'

The mayor rejoined Maigret, pausing en route to shake the harbourmaster's hand with a murmured greeting.

'How are you?'

'Fine, sir.'

'Where were we, inspector? Ah! What's all this I hear about a patched-up fractured skull, insanity and so on?'

'Were you a particular friend of Captain Joris?'

'He was in my employ for twenty-eight years, a fine man, assiduous in his duties.'

'Honest?'

'Almost all my employees are.'

'What was his salary?'

'That would depend, because of the war, which disrupted things everywhere. Enough for him to buy his little house, in any case. And I wager he had at least twenty thousand francs in the bank.'

'No more?'

'Oh, perhaps five thousand francs or so more, at most.'

The upstream lock-gate was opening to let the steamer into the canal; another ship, coming down from Caen, would take its place and head out to sea.

The day was beautifully calm. Everyone was watching Maigret and the mayor. Up on their ship, the English sailors glanced nonchalantly at the crowd while going about their duties.

'What is your opinion of Julie Legrand?'

The mayor hesitated for a moment before grumbling, 'A silly creature who had her head turned because Joris treated her far too nicely. She thinks she's . . . How shall I . . . Anyway, she fancies herself better than she is.'

'And her brother?'

'Never laid eyes on him. I'm told he's a scoundrel.'

They had left the lock behind and were approaching Joris' front gate, where a few kids were still playing and hoping to see some interesting developments.

'What did the captain die of?'

'Strychnine!'

Maigret was wearing his most pigheaded expression. He walked slowly, hands in his pockets, pipe clenched in his teeth. And this pipe seemed to match his big face, for it held a quarter-packet's worth of shag tobacco.

The white cat, stretched full-length in the sunshine atop the garden wall, leaped down in a flash as the two men arrived.

'You're not going in?' asked the mayor in surprise when Maigret stopped short at the cottage gate.

'Just a moment. In your opinion, was Julie the captain's mistress?'

'How would I know that!' exclaimed Monsieur Grand-maison impatiently.

'Did you often visit the captain here?'

'Never! Joris was one of my employees. So you see . . .' And he smiled in what he imagined to be a lordly manner. 'If it's all the same to you, inspector, we'll deal with this as swiftly as possible. I'm expecting guests for lunch.'

'Are you married?'

Frowning in concentration, Maigret kept pursuing his thought, his hand still on the front-gate latch.

Monsieur Grandmaison, who was just over six feet tall, looked down at the inspector, who noticed that although the mayor wasn't exactly cross-eyed, his irises were slightly asymmetrical.

'I should warn you, sir,' said the mayor, 'that if you continue to address me in that tone, you might well come to regret it. Now show me what it is you wish me to see.'

And after pushing open the gate himself, he walked up to and through the front door, where the policeman on guard stepped swiftly out of his way.

Through a glass panel in the kitchen door Maigret could see right away that something was amiss: the two women were there, but he did not see Julie.

'Where is she?'

'She went up to her room! Locked herself in and refused to come down.'

'Just like that, out of the blue?'

'She was doing better,' explained the lighthouse-keeper's wife. 'Still crying, but not as hard, and was talking with us a little. I told her she should eat something, so she opened the cupboard . . .'

'And?'

'I don't know . . . She seemed frightened! She dashed up the stairs, and next thing, we heard the key to her bedroom turning in the lock.'

There was nothing in the cupboard but crockery, a few apples in a basket, a dish of marinating herrings and two greasy plates that had probably held some cold meat.

'I am still waiting!' snapped the mayor, who had stayed out in the front hall. 'It is eleven thirty. What that young woman has been up to should hardly . . .'

Maigret locked the cupboard, pocketed the key and walked heavily to the stairs.

3. The Kitchen Cupboard

'Julie, open up!'

No reply, but the sound of someone collapsing on a bed.

'Open this door!'

Nothing. So Maigret slammed his shoulder into the door – and the screws popped out of the lock plate.

'Why didn't you open the door?'

She was not crying. She was not agitated. No, she was curled up on her bed staring fixedly straight in front of her. When the inspector came too close, she jumped down and attempted to reach the door.

'Leave me alone!' she said loudly.

'Well then, give me the note, Julie.'

'What note?'

She spoke aggressively, hoping to camouflage her lie.

'Did the captain allow your brother to come and visit you?'

No answer.

'Which means that he did not permit it! Your brother used to come and see you anyway. It seems he came here the night Joris disappeared . . .'

A hard, almost hateful look.

'The *Saint-Michel* was in that day. So it was only natural that he would come and see you. One question: when he comes, he usually has something to eat, doesn't he?'

'You're horrible!' she muttered between her teeth.

'And he came here while you were in Paris. Not finding you at home, he left you a note. To make sure that no one else but you would find it, he left it in the kitchen cupboard. Now give me the note . . .'

'I don't have it any more!'

Maigret looked at the empty fireplace, the closed window.

'Give it to me!'

She was rigid in protest, but not like an intelligent woman would be, and she so resembled an angry child that the inspector, catching one of her outraged looks, grumbled softly, 'Silly goose!'

The note was simply under her pillow, where Julie had been lying a minute before. Instead of giving up, however, she went back on the attack, trying to snatch the note from the inspector with a fury that amused him.

Pinioning her hands, he said sternly, 'Are you done now?'

And he read these lines of wretched handwriting, riddled with mistakes.

If you comm back with yor boss be carefull with him for theres bad fellos that have got it in for him. I wil be back in 2 or 3 days with the ship. Dont look for the cuttletts I ate them. Yor brother for life.

Maigret bowed his head, thrown so off-balance that he paid no further attention to Julie.

Fifteen minutes later, Captain Delcourt was telling him that the *Saint-Michel* was probably in Fécamp and that if the north-westerly winds held steady, the ship would arrive the following night.

'Do you know the position of every single vessel?'

And Maigret, uneasy, looked out at the shimmering sea, with only a single plume of smoke visible in the distance.

'The ports are all in contact with one another,' replied the harbourmaster. 'Look! There is the list of all the ships due in today.'

He pointed to a blackboard hanging on the wall of the office, with the list written out in chalk.

'Have you discovered something? Well, don't rely too much on what people say. Even important people! If you only knew how much petty jealousy can flourish around here . . .'

After waving to the captain of a freighter heading out to sea, the harbourmaster looked out of his office window at the Buvette de la Marine and sighed.

'You'll see . . .'

By three o'clock, the officials from the public prosecutor's office had finished their work. A dozen or so men filed out of Joris' cottage and walked through the little green gate towards the four cars that awaited them, surrounded by onlookers.

The deputy public prosecutor gazed around him appreciatively.

'The duck hunting here must be superb!' he remarked to Monsieur Grandmaison.

'We've had a disappointing season. But last year—'

The mayor suddenly dashed over to the first car as it was pulling away.

'You'll all stop in at my house for a moment, I hope? My wife will be expecting us . . .'

When Maigret was the only man left, the mayor turned to him with just enough bonhomie to appear polite.

'Ride back with us, inspector. You are invited as well, naturally.'

Only Julie and the two women remained in Captain Joris' cottage, along with the local policeman at the door, to await the hearse that would deliver the body to Caen.

The atmosphere in the cars had already taken on the festive air that often enlivens the trip when convivial companions return from a funeral. While Maigret perched uncomfortably on a jump seat, the mayor was chatting with the deputy public prosecutor.

'If it were up to me, I would stay here all year round, but my wife is not that fond of country living. So we spend most of our time at our house in Caen – although my wife has only just got back from Juan-les-Pins, where she spent a month with the children.'

'How old is your boy now?'

'Fifteen.'

The lock workers watched the cars drive by. And almost immediately, on the road to Lion-sur-Mer, they arrived at the mayor's residence, a large Norman villa on a property surrounded by white fencing and strewn with animal lawn ornaments.

Standing in the front hall in a dark silk dress, Madame Grandmaison welcomed her guests with the delicately aloof smile befitting her station in life. The drawing room was at their disposal; cigars and liqueurs were set out on a table in the smoking room.

All these people knew one another. The social elite of Caen were having a reunion. A maid in a white apron took everyone's hats and coats.

'Really, judge: you've never visited Ouistreham – and you've lived in Caen for *how* long?'

'Twelve years, dear madame . . . Ah! Here's Mademoiselle Gisèle!'

A girl of fourteen had come in to curtsey slightly to the guests, already holding herself like quite the lady – and, like her mother, acutely conscious of her social position. Meanwhile, however, no one had remembered to introduce Maigret to the mistress of the house.

Turning to the deputy public prosecutor, that lady inquired, 'I suppose that after what you've all just been through you would prefer something a little stronger than tea? A liqueur brandy, then? . . . And your wife, is she still in Fontainebleau?'

Everywhere, people were talking. Maigret heard snatches of conversations.

'No, ten ducks per night is the limit . . . But I assure you, it isn't cold at all! The blind is heated . . .'

On another side: '. . . hit hard by the drop in business?'

'That depends on the company. Here we've been relatively unaffected. Locally, none of our vessels is in trouble. The smaller concerns, on the other hand, especially those with only schooners for the coastal trade, are beginning to suffer. I might even say that those companies depending

39

on schooners are in general looking to sell them, for they cannot cover their expenses . . .'

'No, madame,' insisted the deputy public prosecutor soothingly, 'there is no reason for alarm. The mystery – if there is one – of this man's death will soon be resolved. Isn't that so, inspector? . . . But . . . Haven't you been introduced? May I present Detective Chief Inspector Maigret, a man of stellar reputation from the Police Judiciaire.'

Maigret stood stiffly with a most unwelcoming expression on his face, and when young Gisèle smilingly held out to him a plate of petits fours, he gave her an odd look.

'No, thank you.'

'Really? You don't like cakes?'

'To your good health!'

'Here's to our charming hostess!'

The public prosecutor, a tall, thin man of about fifty who could barely see through the thick lenses of his glasses, now took Maigret aside.

'I'm giving you carte blanche, of course. But telephone me every evening to keep me up to date. What do you think of this case? A sordid affair, is it not?' Noticing Monsieur Grandmaison approaching, he added in a louder voice, 'And besides, you are lucky to be dealing with a mayor like Grandmaison here, who will be of great assistance in your inquiry. Is that not so, dear friend? I was just telling the inspector . . .'

'If he wants,' replied the mayor, 'we'd be delighted to have him stay in our house. I suppose you are at present at the hotel?'

'I am,' replied the inspector, 'and thank you for your invitation, but the hotel is so conveniently situated . . .'

'And you believe you will ferret something out at the tavern? A word of warning, inspector! You don't know Ouistreham! Consider what people who spend their lives in a tavern can conjure up through sheer imagination! They'd point the finger at their own parents simply to have a good tale to tell.'

'Why don't we talk about something else?' suggested Madame Grandmaison with a gracious smile. 'Inspector, a petit four? . . . Really? . . . You don't like sweets?'

For the second time! Unbelievable! And Maigret was almost moved to pull out his big fat pipe in protest.

'If you will excuse me. There are some matters I must attend to.'

No one tried to detain him. All things considered, they were no more enamoured of his presence than he was of theirs. Outside, he filled his pipe and walked slowly back to the harbour. The local people knew him now, knew that he had stood a round of drinks at the bar, so they greeted him with a hint of friendliness.

As he approached the quay, he noticed the hearse carrying the captain's body drive away towards Caen and saw Julie's face, framed in a downstairs window at the cottage. The other women were trying to cajole her back into the kitchen.

A fishing boat had just come in, and people gathered around it as the two fishermen sorted out their catch. The customs officials up on the bridge parapet whiled away the slow hours of their shift.

'I've just had a confirmation!' called out Captain Delcourt, hurrying over to Maigret. 'The *Saint-Michel* will arrive tomorrow! She was laid up for three days in Fécamp having her bowsprit repaired.'

'Say, tell me: does she ever carry salted cod's roe as cargo?'

'Cod's roe? No. The Norwegian roe comes in on Scandinavian schooners or small steamers. They don't unload at Caen, though, they make directly for the sardine ports, like Concarneau, Les Sables-d'Olonne, Saint-Jean-de-Luz . . .'

'What about seal oil?'

This time the captain stared at him in surprise.

'Why would they carry that?'

'I don't really know . . .'

'The answer's no, in any case. These coasters almost always carry the same cargo: vegetables, and onions in particular, for England, coal for the Breton ports, stone, cement, slates . . . By the way, I asked some lock workers about the *Saint-Michel*'s last call here. On the 16th of September, she came in from Caen at the tail end of the tide, when everyone was about to go off duty. Joris pointed out that the water in the channel was too low for safe access to the sea, especially when it was so foggy. The skipper insisted on going through the lock anyway, though, so that he could leave the next morning at first light. She spent the night here, in the outer harbour, moored to some pilings. At low tide, they were high and dry, couldn't leave until nine the next morning.'

'And Julie's brother was aboard?'

'He must have been! There were only three of them: the skipper, who also owns the boat, and two crew. Big Louis—'

'He's the ex-convict?'

'Yes. He's called Big Louis because he's big, bigger than you are and could strangle a man with one hand . . .'

'A bad sort?'

'If you ask the mayor or anyone well-to-do in these parts, they'll say yes. Me, I never knew him before he went off to prison. He doesn't turn up here very often. All I know is, he has never caused any trouble in Ouistreham. He does drink, of course. Although . . . It's difficult to tell, he always seems half-soused. He hangs around the harbour. He's gimpy in one leg and his head and shoulders are hunched to one side, which makes him look a bit shifty. Still, the skipper of the *Saint-Michel* is happy enough with him.'

'He was here yesterday, while his sister was in Paris.'

Not daring to deny it, Captain Delcourt looked away. And Maigret understood then and there that there was a fraternal bond among these men of the sea, that they would never tell him all they knew.

'He's not the only one . . .'

'What do you mean?'

'Nothing, really. I heard about a stranger seen prowling around . . . But nothing definite.'

'Who saw him?'

'I don't know. People talk, that's all . . . Could you manage a quick drink?'

For the second time, Maigret settled into the bar, where he was welcomed with handshakes.

'Well! Those gentlemen from the public prosecutor's office certainly got their job done in a hurry.'

'What's your pleasure?'

'I'll have a beer.'

The sun had been out all day long. But now streamers of mist were threading their way from tree to tree, and vapour began rising from the canal.

'Another pea-souper,' sighed the captain.

And at the same instant, they heard the fog horn.

'It's the light buoy, out at the entrance to the harbour channel.'

'Did Captain Joris go often to Norway?' asked Maigret abruptly.

'When he sailed for the Compagnie Anglo-Normande, yes! Especially right after the war, when there was a shortage of wood. It's a lousy cargo, wood is – gets in the way of handling the ship.'

'Did you work for the same company?'

'Not for long. I was mostly with Worms, in Bordeaux. I ran the "ferry", we called it, just the one run: Bordeaux to Nantes, Nantes to Bordeaux. For eighteen years!'

'What's Julie's background?'

'A fishing family, Port-en-Bessin. If you can call them fisherfolk . . . The father never did much of anything. Died during the war. The mother must still be peddling fish in the streets, when she isn't swilling red wine in bistros . . .'

For the second time, thinking of Julie, Maigret smiled to himself. He remembered her arriving in his office in Paris, neat as a pin in her blue suit, a determined little thing . . .

44

And that very morning, when she struggled so clumsily, like a child, to keep him from taking her brother's letter.

Joris' house was already fading into the mist. There was no light any more upstairs, where the body had lain, or in the dining room, only the light in the front hall and probably at the back of the house, in the kitchen, where the two women were keeping Julie company.

Some lock workers now came in from the harbour but, sizing up the situation, went off to a table in the back to play some dominoes. The lighthouse lit up.

'The same again!' called the captain, pointing to the glasses. 'This one's on me.'

When Maigret asked the next question, his voice sounded strangely soft, almost velvety.

'If Joris were alive right now, where would he be? Here?'

'No! At home. In his slippers.'

'In the dining room? In his bedroom?'

'In the kitchen. With the evening paper. And then he'd read one of those books on gardening. He'd fallen head over heels for flowers. Just look at his garden! Still full of them, although it's late in the season.'

The other men laughed, but were a trifle chagrined at not having a passion for flowers instead of haunting their beloved tavern.

'He never went hunting?'

'Not often . . . A few times, when he was invited.'

'With the mayor?'

'When the shooting was good, they'd go off to the duck blind together.'

The place was so poorly lit that it was difficult to see the domino players through the smoky haze. A big stove made the air even heavier. Outside, it was almost evening, but the fog turned this darkness more oppressive, almost sinister. The fog horn was still sounding. Maigret's pipe made faint sizzling noises.

Leaning back in his chair, he half closed his eyes, trying to piece together his scattered clues floating in a formless mass.

'Joris vanished for six weeks only to return with a cracked and patched-up skull,' he murmured, without realizing that he was speaking out loud.

Then poison is waiting for him on the day he comes home!

And Julie doesn't find her brother's note in the pantry cupboard until the next day . . .

Maigret heaved a great sigh and muttered, 'So: someone tried to kill him. Then someone got him back on his feet. Then someone finished him off. Unless . . .'

For these three statements did not fit together. Then he had an outlandish idea, so outlandish that it startled him.

'Unless this someone wasn't trying to kill him that first time? And was only trying to affect his reason?'

Hadn't the doctors in Paris affirmed that his operation could only have been performed by a highly skilled surgeon?

But does one fracture a man's skull to steal away his mind?

And besides! What proof was there that Joris had lost his mind for ever?

The others watched Maigret in respectful silence. The customs official simply signalled to the waitress for another round.

And they sat off in their corners in the fug of the tavern, each in a reverie slightly blurred by drink.

They heard three cars go by: the public prosecutor's party was returning to Caen after the Grandmaisons' reception. By now Captain Joris' body was already in a cold room at the Institut Médico-Légal.

No one spoke. Dominoes clicked on the unvarnished wooden table. The puzzling crime, it seemed, had gradually come to weigh heavily on everyone's mind. They felt it hanging, almost visibly, over their heads. Their faces creased into scowls.

The youngest of the customs officials grew so uneasy that he rose and blurted out, 'Time I was getting home to the little woman . . .'

Maigret handed his tobacco pouch to his neighbour, who filled his pipe and passed the tobacco along. Then Delcourt stood up as well to escape the now oppressive atmosphere.

'How much does it come to, Marthe?'

'These two rounds? Nine francs seventy-five. And the gentleman's from yesterday, that's three francs ten.'

Everyone was on his feet. Moist air swept in through the open door. There were handshakes all around.

Once outside, the men strode off into the mist in every direction, as the fog horn boomed over the sound of their footsteps.

Maigret stood listening to all the footsteps heading off in every direction. Heavy footsteps, sometimes pausing, or suddenly darting away . . .

And he realized that somehow there was now fear in

the air. They were afraid, all those men going home, afraid of nothing, of everything, of some nebulous danger, some unforeseeable disaster, afraid of the dark and the lights in the mist.

'What if it isn't over?'

Maigret knocked the ashes from his pipe and buttoned his overcoat.

4. *The* Saint-Michel

'Do you like it?' inquired the hotel-owner anxiously about each dish.

'It's fine! Fine!' replied the inspector, who wasn't actually quite sure what he was eating.

He was alone in a hotel dining room spacious enough for forty or fifty guests. The hotel was for Ouistreham's summer visitors. The furniture was the kind found in any seaside hotel. On the tables, small vases of flowers.

No connection at all with the Ouistreham that the inspector found interesting and was beginning to understand.

That was what pleased him. What he hated the most, in an inquiry, were the first steps, with all the attendant false moves and misinterpretations.

The word Ouistreham, for example. In Paris, it had conjured up a complete fantasy, a port city like Saint-Malo. The evening he arrived, Maigret had decided that it was really a forbidding hole full of gruff, taciturn people.

Now he had got his bearings. Felt more at home. Ouistreham was an ordinary village at the end of a bit of road planted with small trees. What truly counted was the harbour: a lock, a lighthouse, Joris' cottage, the Buvette de la Marine.

And the workaday rhythm of this harbour as well: the

twice-daily tides, the fishermen lugging their baskets, the handful of men exclusively devoted to the constant traffic through the lock.

Some words now meant more to Maigret: captain, freighter, coaster. He was watching all that in action and learning the rules of the game.

The mystery had not been resolved. He still could not explain the things that had stymied him from the first. But at least now the cast of characters was clear: all were accounted for, with their settings and little everyday routines.

'Will you be staying here long?' asked the hotel-owner as he served the coffee himself.

'That I don't know.'

'If this had happened during the season it would have hit us hard.'

Now Maigret could distinguish among precisely four Ouistrehams: the Harbour, the Village, the Villas, the Seaside Resort – this last temporarily on holiday itself.

'You're going out, inspector?'

'Just a stroll before bedtime.'

The tide was almost full in. The weather was much colder than it had been; the fog, while still opaque, was turning into droplets of icy water.

Everything was dark. Everything was closed. Only the misty eye of the lighthouse was visible. And up on the lock, voices called to one another.

A short blast from a ship's whistle. A green light and a red one drawing near; a mass gliding along, level with the wall . . .

Maigret had learned the drill. A steamer was coming in.

The shadowy figure now approaching would pick up the hawser and secure it to the nearest bollard. Then, up on the bridge, the captain would give the order to reverse engines.

Delcourt passed close by the inspector, looking anxiously out towards the jetties.

'What's going on?'

'I can't tell . . .'

The harbourmaster squinted hard, as if it were possible to see into the pitch dark through sheer force of will. Two men were already moving to close the lock-gates.

'Wait a minute!' Delcourt yelled to them.

And exclaimed in astonishment:

'It's them!'

Just then a voice not fifty metres away called out, 'Hey there! Louis! Down jib and stand by to come alongside port side-to . . .'

The voice had come from the darkness below, over by the jetties. A firefly of light was coming closer. Someone seemed to be moving around; canvas fell as rings clattered along a stay.

Then a mainsail slipped past, close enough to touch.

'How in heaven did they pull that off!' grumbled Delcourt, who then turned towards the schooner and yelled, 'Get her nose in under the port quarter of the steamer, so's we can close the gates!'

A man had leaped ashore with a mooring line and now stood looking around him, hands on his hips.

'The *Saint-Michel*?' Maigret asked Delcourt.

'The same . . . They must have flown over the water.'

There was only a small lantern down on the schooner's deck, illuminating a confused scene: a cask, a pile of gear, the silhouette of a man leaving the tiller to dash forwards to the schooner's bows.

The lock workers seemed particularly interested in the boat, arriving one after the other to take a look at it.

'The lock-gate winches, men! Back to work! Let's go!'

With the gates closed, water roared in through the sluices, and both vessels began to rise. The lantern's pale light drew closer. As the schooner's deck drew level with the quay, the man there hailed the harbourmaster.

'All's well?'

'All's well,' replied Delcourt guardedly. 'Didn't expect you so soon!'

'Had the wind at our backs, and Louis put up all the canvas we had. We even left a freighter in our wake!'

'Heading for Caen?'

'We'll be unloading there, yes. Anything new around here?'

Maigret was a few paces away, Big Louis a bit further off, but they could barely see each other. Only Delcourt and the *Saint-Michel*'s captain were talking, and now the harbourmaster, at a loss, looked over at Maigret.

'I heard it's in the paper that Joris has come back. Is that true?'

'He came back and he left again,' replied Delcourt.

'What do you mean?'

Big Louis had taken a step closer. With his hands in his pockets and the one shoulder crooked, he looked rather flabby in the darkness, like a shapeless hulk.

'He's dead . . .'

Now Big Louis went right up to Delcourt.

'Is that true?' he grunted.

Hearing his voice for the first time, Maigret found that flabby, too, in a way: hoarse, and somewhat drawling. He still could not see his face.

'The first night he was home,' explained Delcourt, 'he was poisoned. And here,' he quickly pointed out, 'is the inspector from Paris who's in charge of the case.'

Having worried for some time how to prudently reveal this information, the harbourmaster now seemed relieved. Had he been afraid the men of the *Saint-Michel* might accidentally get themselves into trouble?

'Ah! So this gentleman is with the police . . .'

The schooner was still rising. Her skipper swung his legs over the rails and dropped down on to the quay, but then hesitated before shaking hands with Maigret.

'Hard to imagine . . .' he said slowly, still thinking about Joris.

He seemed worried as well, and even more obviously than Delcourt.

Louis, his tall form swaying, his head tilted to one side, barked out something the inspector could not understand.

'What did he say?'

'He was grumbling in dialect. He said: "a filthy business"!'

'What was a filthy business?' the inspector asked the ex-convict, but Big Louis simply looked him in the eye. They had moved closer and could now see each other's faces. Big Louis' features looked swollen; one cheek was

53

bigger than the other, or simply seemed so because of the way he always tilted his head to one side. Puffy flesh, and big eyes that seemed to start from his head.

'You were here yesterday!' said the inspector sharply.

The water was at the proper level; the upper gates were opening. The steamer moved smoothly into the canal, and Delcourt hurried over to record her tonnage and provenance.

A voice shouted down from the bridge: 'Nine hundred tons! . . . Rouen!'

The *Saint-Michel* remained in the lock, however, and each of the men stationed there to deal with her, aware that something unusual was happening, waited, wrapped in shadows, listening carefully.

Delcourt returned, writing the necessary information in his notebook.

'Well?' asked Maigret impatiently.

'Well, what?' grumbled Louis. 'You says I was here yesterday! That's 'cause I was . . .'

It was hard to understand him, because he had a peculiar way of chewing on his words with his mouth almost closed, as if he were eating. Not to mention his thick local accent . . .

'Why did you come here?'

'See my sister.'

'And, not finding her at home, you left her a note.'

In the meantime, Maigret was stealthily observing the schooner's captain, who was dressed just like Louis. There was nothing special about him; indeed, he seemed more like a seasoned bosun's mate than the skipper of a coaster.

'We were three days at Fécamp for repairs,' the man now piped up, 'so Louis grabbed his chance to come here and see Julie!'

All around the lock, the men on duty must have been straining to listen in, keeping as quiet as possible. The fog horn still moaned in the distance, and the fog itself was growing wetter, leaving the cobblestones black and gleaming.

A hatchway opened in the schooner's deck, and a man's head emerged, with unkempt hair and a bushy beard.

'What's wrong? Why're we sitting here?'

'Shut it, Célestin!' said his skipper quickly.

Delcourt was stamping up and down the quay to warm himself up – and perhaps to save face as well, for he didn't know if he should stay there or not.

'Louis, what made you think that Joris was in danger?'

'Huh!' said Louis, and shrugged. 'He'd already had his skull stove in, hadn't he, so it wasn't hard to work out.'

It was so difficult to make out the syllables all mashed together in the man's grunting that Maigret could have done with an interpreter.

The atmosphere felt intensely uncomfortable and in a way, mysteriously threatening.

Louis looked towards the cottage but couldn't see a thing, not even a darker patch in the night.

'She's there, our Julie?'

'Yes. Are you going to go and see her?'

Louis shook his head with big sweeps, like a bear.

'Why not?'

'Sure she'll cry.'

It sounded like 'Shore shale crah' – and in the disgusted tone of a man who can't take the sight of tears.

They were still standing there; the fog was thickening, soaking their shoulders, and Delcourt decided to intervene.

'Anyone for a drink?'

A lock worker chimed in, off at his post in the darkness.

'They just closed the bar!'

'We could go below to the cabin, if you like,' offered the *Saint-Michel*'s captain.

There were four of them: Maigret, Delcourt, Big Louis and the skipper, whose name was Lannec. The cabin wasn't large, and the small stove gave off heat so intense that the air was hazy with humidity. The paraffin lamp, set in gimbals, looked almost red hot.

Cabin walls of varnished pitch pine. A scarred oak table, so worn that the entire surface was uneven. Dirty dishes still sat out, along with some sturdy but gummy-looking glasses and a half-bottle of red.

On either side of the cabin were wide, rectangular recesses, like cupboards without doors, for the beds of the captain and Louis, the first mate. Unmade beds, with dirty boots and clothing tossed on to them. Whiffs of tar, alcohol, cooking and stuffy bedrooms, but most of all, that indescribable smell of a boat.

Everyone looked less unsettling in the lamplight. Lannec had a brown moustache and sharp, bright eyes. He had taken a bottle from a locker and was rinsing glasses by filling them with water he then poured out on the floor.

'It seems that you were here on the night of the 16th of September, Captain Lannec.'

Big Louis was sitting hunched over with his elbows on the table.

'Right, we were here,' replied Lannec, pouring out the drinks.

'Wasn't that unusual? Because spending the night in the outer harbour would mean you'd have to keep an eye on your moorings, because of the tide.'

'It happens,' said Lannec casually.

'Like that you can often get underway a few hours earlier in the morning,' added Delcourt, who seemed determined to keep things cordial.

'Captain Joris didn't come and see you aboard?'

'While we were in the lock . . . Not later on.'

'And you neither saw nor heard anything out of the ordinary?'

'Cheers! . . . No, nothing.'

'You, Louis, you went to bed?'

'Must have.'

'What's that?'

'I said must have . . . Was some time ago.'

'You didn't visit your sister?'

'Mebbe so. Not for long . . .'

'Didn't Joris forbid you to set foot in his house?'

'Bunk!'

'What do you mean by that?'

'Nothing. It's all rubbish . . . You finished with me now?'

Maigret couldn't really charge him with anything. Besides, he had no desire at all to arrest him.

'Finished for today.'

Louis spoke with his skipper in Breton, rose, emptied his glass and touched his cap in farewell.

'What did he say to you?' asked the inspector.

'That I didn't need him on the Caen run, so he'll rejoin me back here after I've delivered our cargo.'

'Where is he going?'

'He didn't tell me.'

Delcourt hurried to look out of the hatchway, listened for a little while and returned.

'He's over on the dredger.'

'The what?'

'You didn't notice the two dredgers in the canal? They're simply moored there for the moment. They have sleeping quarters there. Sailors would rather kip on an old boat than in a hotel.'

'Another round?'

And after looking intently about the cabin, Maigret made himself more comfortable.

'What was your first port of call after leaving Ouistreham, on the 16th of last month?'

'Southampton. Delivering a cargo of stone.'

'Then?'

'Boulogne.'

'You haven't been up to Norway since then?'

'I've been there only once, six years ago.'

'Did you know Joris well?'

'Us, we know everyone, you see. From La Rochelle to Rotterdam. Cheers! . . . In fact, this here is good Dutch gin I got in Holland. Cigar?'

He took a box from a drawer.

'Cigars that cost ten cents over there. One franc!'

They were fat, smoothly rolled with gold bands.

'It's strange,' sighed Maigret. 'I was told that Joris definitely came aboard your boat when you were in the outer harbour, and that someone else was with him.'

Lannec was busy cutting the tip of his cigar, however, and when he looked up, his face wore no expression.

'I wouldn't have any reason to hide that.'

Outside, someone jumped on to the bridge with a loud thud. A head appeared at the top of the hatchway ladder.

'The steamer from Le Havre's coming in!'

Delcourt sprang up and turned to Maigret.

'I have to clear the lock for her, so the *Saint-Michel* will be moving out.'

'I assume I may continue my run?' added the captain.

'To Caen?'

'Yes. The canal doesn't go anywhere else! We'll probably be finished unloading by tomorrow evening.'

They all seemed like honest men, all had frank, open faces, and yet everything about them rang false! But so subtly that Maigret couldn't have said what or where the trouble was.

Lannec, Delcourt, Joris, everyone at the Buvette de la Marine, they appeared to be the salt of the earth. And even Big Louis, the ex-con, hadn't made such a bad impression!

'Don't get up, Lannec, I'll cast off for you,' said the harbourmaster, and went topside to clear the hawser from its bollard. Célestin, the old fellow who had stuck his head up out of the fo'c'sle, now hobbled across the deck muttering, 'That Big Louis, he's 'scaped off again!'

And after letting out both the jib and flying jib, he poled the schooner off with a boat hook. Maigret leaped ashore just in time. The mist had definitely turned to rain, making the men at work, the harbour lights and the steamer from Le Havre, now whistling with impatience in the lock, visible once again.

Winches clanked; water raced through the open sluices. The schooner's mainsail blocked the view up the canal. From the lock bridge, Maigret could make out the two dredgers, great ugly boats with complicated shapes and grim upper works encrusted with rust. He made his way over there with great care because the surrounding area was strewn with junk, old cables, anchors and scrap iron. He was walking along a plank used as a gangway when he saw a light glimmering through a split seam in the hulk.

'Big Louis!' he called.

The light vanished immediately. Louis' head and torso emerged from a hatchway missing its cover.

'What d'you want?'

But as he spoke something was moving below him, in the belly of the dredger. A vague shape was slipping away with the utmost caution. The sheet iron was echoing with knocks and bumps . . .

'Who's that with you?'

'With me? Here?'

When Maigret tried to look around, he almost plummeted into a metre or so of slimy mud, stagnating in the hold of the dredger.

Someone had definitely been there, but he was long gone: the banging noises were now coming from a different part of the vessel. And the inspector wasn't sure where he might safely walk. He was completely unfamiliar with the mess decks of this apocalyptic boat – and now banged his head smartly against one of the dredger's buckets.

'You've got nothing to say?'

An indistinct grunt. This seemed to mean, 'I don't know what you're talking about.'

To search the two dredgers at night, the inspector would have needed ten men – men who knew their way around them, too! Maigret beat a retreat. The rain made voices carry surprisingly far, and he could hear someone in the harbour saying, '. . . lying right across the channel.'

He followed the voice. It was the first mate of the steamer from Le Havre, who was pointing out something to Delcourt. And the harbourmaster seemed quite disconcerted when Maigret showed up.

'It's hard to believe they'd lose it and never notice,' the mate went on.

'Lose what?' asked the inspector.

'The dinghy.'

'What dinghy?'

'This one here, that we bumped into just inside the jetties. It belongs to the schooner that was ahead of us. Her name is on the stern: *Saint-Michel*.'

'It must have come loose,' observed Delcourt dismissively. 'That happens!'

'It did not come loose, for the very good reason that in

this weather, the dinghy would not have been in tow, but on deck!'

And the lock workers, still at their posts, were trying to hear every word.

'We'll see about it in the morning. Leave the dinghy here.'

Turning to Maigret, Delcourt gave him a crooked smile.

'You can see what an odd sort of job I have,' he murmured. 'There's always something . . .'

Maigret did not smile back, however. In fact, he replied with the utmost gravity.

'Listen: if you don't see me anywhere tomorrow morning at seven, or perhaps eight, then telephone the public prosecutor at Caen.'

'But what . . .'

'Goodnight! And make sure that the dinghy does stay here.'

To lay a false trail, he walked off along the jetty, hands in his pockets, his overcoat collar turned up. The sea rumbled and sighed beneath his feet, ahead of him, on his right, on his left. The air he breathed into his lungs smelled strongly of iodine.

When almost at the end of the jetty, he bent down to pick something up.

5. Notre-Dame-des-Dunes

At dawn Maigret plodded back to the Hôtel de l'Univers in his sodden overcoat with a parched throat, having smoked pipe after pipe. The hotel seemed deserted but he found the hotel-owner in the kitchen, lighting the fire.

'You were out all night?'

'Yes. Would you bring some coffee up to my room as soon as possible? Oh, and is there any way I can have a bath?'

'I'll have to fire up the boiler.'

'Then don't bother.'

A grey morning with the inevitable fog, but it was a light, luminous one. Maigret's eyelids were stinging, and his head felt empty as he stood at the open window in his room, waiting for the coffee.

A strange night. He had done nothing sensational. Made no great discoveries. Yet he had made progress in his understanding of the crime. Many nuggets of information had been added to his growing store.

The arrival of the *Saint-Michel*. Lannec's behaviour. Was the skipper's attitude ambiguous? Dubious? Not even that! Yet he was a slippery fellow. But Delcourt as well was sometimes less than forthcoming. They all were, if they had anything to do with this harbour! Big Louis, for example, was definitely acting suspiciously. He hadn't gone on to

Caen with the schooner. He was holed up on an empty dredger. And Maigret was sure that he wasn't there alone.

Then he had learned that the *Saint-Michel* had lost its dinghy shortly before entering the harbour. And at the end of a jetty, he had made a most unusual find: a gold fountain-pen.

It was a wooden jetty supported by pilings. At its far end, near the green light, an iron ladder went down to the water. The dinghy had been found in that area. In other words, the *Saint-Michel* had been carrying someone who did not want to be seen in Ouistreham. After landing in the dinghy, this passenger had let it drift away, and, as he had leaned over at the top of the ladder to hoist himself on to the jetty, the gold fountain-pen had slipped from his pocket.

The man had taken refuge in the dredger, where Louis was to join him.

This scenario was just about airtight. There could be no other interpretation of the facts.

Conclusion: an unknown man was hiding in Ouistreham. He had not come here without a reason: he had a job to do. And he belonged to a milieu in which men used gold fountain-pens!

So: not a sailor. Not a tramp . . . The expensive pen suggested clothing of equally good quality. The man must be a gentleman – a 'gent' as they say in the countryside . . . And off-season, in Ouistreham, a 'gent' would not pass unnoticed. He would have to lie low all day in the dredger. But wouldn't he come out at night to accomplish whatever he had come here for?

Maigret had therefore resigned himself, grumpily, to mounting guard. A job for a junior inspector! Spending

hours in the drizzle peering at the inordinately complicated shadows of the dredger.

Nothing had happened. No one had come ashore. Day
had dawned, and now the inspector was furious at not
being able to enjoy a hot bath. Contemplating his bed, he
considered snatching a few hours' rest.

The hotel-owner came in with his coffee.

'You're not going to sleep?'

'I haven't decided yet. Would you take a telegram to the
post office for me?'

He was summoning Lucas, a trusted colleague, for
Maigret had no desire to keep an eye on the dredger again
that night.

The window looked out on the harbour, Joris' cottage and
the sandbanks now emerging as the ebb tide left the bay.

While the inspector wrote his telegram, the hotel-owner
looked outside, remarking off-handedly, 'Well! Captain
Joris' maid is going for a walk . . .'

Looking up, Maigret saw Julie, who closed the front gate
and set out briskly for the beach.

'What's over there?'

'What do you mean?'

'Where can one go? Are there any houses?'

'Nothing at all! Only the beach, but no one goes there
because it's interrupted by breakwaters and mud sinkholes.'

'No path or road?'

'No. You reach the mouth of the Orne, and the banks
are marshy all along the river. Wait, now . . . There are
some duck blinds there for hunting.'

Maigret was already heading out of the door with a

determined frown. He strode across the lock bridge, and by the time he reached the beach Julie was just a few hundred metres ahead of him.

The place was deserted. The only living creatures in the morning mist were the gulls, shrieking as they flew. To avoid being seen, the inspector went up into the dunes on his right.

The air was cool and the sea, calm. The white hem of the surf subsided with a rhythm like breathing and the crunching of broken shells.

Julie was not out for a walk. She advanced quickly, holding her little black coat tightly closed. She hadn't had time, since Joris' death, to order mourning clothes, so she was wearing all her black or dark things: an old-fashioned coat, woollen stockings, a hat with a downturned brim.

She staggered along, her feet sinking into the soft sand. Twice she turned around but did not see Maigret, hidden by the rolling dunes.

About a kilometre from Ouistreham, however, she almost spotted him when she went abruptly off to the right.

Maigret had thought she was making for a duck blind, but there was nothing like that out in the landscape of sand and coarse beach grass.

Nothing but a tumbledown structure missing one entire wall. Facing the ocean, five metres in from the high-tide line, there was a small chapel, probably constructed a few centuries earlier.

It had a semicircular vault, and the missing wall allowed Maigret to judge the thickness of the others: almost one metre of solid stone.

Julie went inside to the back of the chapel, and the

inspector could now hear small objects being moved, almost certainly shells, from the sound of them.

He moved forwards cautiously and could see a small recess in the far wall, closed with a metal grille. Beneath was a kind of tiny altar, over which hovered Julie, looking for something.

She whipped around and recognized Maigret, who had had no time to hide.

'What are you doing here?' she exclaimed.

'And you?'

'I . . . I've come to pray to Notre-Dame-des-Dunes . . .'

She was nervous, and everything about her showed that she was hiding something. Her red eyes betrayed an almost sleepless night, and two locks of untidy hair stuck out from beneath her hat.

'Ah! This place is a Lady chapel?'

And indeed, in the niche behind the grille was a statue of the Virgin, so old and eaten away by time that it was almost unrecognizable.

The stone all around the niche was covered with a tangle of supplications written in pencil or incised with a sharp rock or pocket-knife.

Help Denise pass her exam . . . Notre-Dame-des-Dunes, make Jojo quickly learn to read . . . Grant good health to the whole family and especially Grandmother and Grandfather . . .

There were more earthly inscriptions, too, with hearts pierced by arrows.

Robert & Jeanne for ever . . .

Dried stalks that had once been flowers still hung from the grille, but what made this chapel different from so many others were the shells piled high on the ruins of the altar. Shells of every shape and kind, and there were words written on all of them, mostly in pencil, in the clumsy handwriting of children and simple souls, or sometimes the firmer script of more literate supplicants.

May the fishing be good in Newfoundland and Papa need never sign up again . . .

The floor was of beaten earth. Where the wall had fallen, the view was of sandy beach and silvery sea in the white haze. And in spite of herself, having no idea how to handle the situation, Julie kept glancing anxiously at the shells.

'Did you bring one here?' asked Maigret.

Julie shook her head.

'When I arrived, though, you were going through them. What were you looking for?'

'Nothing, I . . .'

'You . . . ?'

'Nothing!'

And she glared stubbornly, clutching her coat more tightly around her.

Now it was the inspector's turn to pick up the shells one by one to read what was written on them. Suddenly, he smiled. On an enormous clam shell he read, 'Notre-Dame-des-Dunes, help my brother Louis succeed so we will all be happy.'

The date on it was 13 September. So this primitive ex-voto had been brought here three days before Captain Joris vanished!

And hadn't Julie come here to remove it?

'Is this what you were hunting for?'

'What business is it of yours?'

Her eyes never left the shell. She seemed ready to jump at Maigret to tear it from his hands.

'Give it to me! Put it back where it belongs!'

'All right, I'll leave it here, but you must, too. Come on, we'll talk about it on the walk back.'

'I've nothing to say to you.'

They set out, leaning forwards because their feet sank into the soft sand. The wind was so sharp that their noses were red and their cheeks gleamed.

'Everything your brother has done has gone wrong, hasn't it?'

She stared straight ahead at the beach.

'Some things are impossible to hide,' he continued. 'I'm not talking only about . . . about what landed him in prison.'

'Of course! It's always that! After twenty years they'll still be saying—'

'No, no, Julie! Louis is a good sailor. Even an excellent one, I hear, able to serve as a first mate. Except that one fine day he gets drunk with some fellows he's just met and does some stupid things, doesn't return to his boat, drags around for weeks without a job. Am I right? At times like that, he asks you for help. You – and just a few weeks ago,

Joris. Then he becomes responsible and hardworking again for a while.'

'So?'

'What was the plan that you wanted, on the 13th of September, to make turn out well?'

Julie stopped and looked into his face. She was much calmer now. She had had time to reflect. And there was an appealing gravity in her eyes.

'I knew it would bring us trouble. And yet, my brother did nothing! I swear to you that if he had killed the captain, I would have been the first to pay him back in kind.'

Her voice was low and heavy with emotion.

'It's just that, there *are* some coincidences, and then that time in prison always hanging around his neck. Whenever anyone does something wrong, Louis gets blamed for everything that happens afterwards.'

'What was the plan Louis had?'

'It wasn't a plan. It was quite simple. He'd met a really rich man, I don't remember any more if it was in England or at Le Havre. He didn't tell me his name. A gentleman who'd had enough of life ashore and wanted to buy a yacht and travel. He asked Louis to find him a boat.'

They were still standing on the beach, where all they could see of Ouistreham was the lighthouse, a raw white tower set off by the paler sky.

'Louis talked to his skipper about it. Because for some time, on account of the slump, Lannec had been wanting to sell the *Saint-Michel*. And that's the whole of it! The *Saint-Michel* is the best coaster anyone could find for turning into a yacht. In the beginning my brother was supposed to get ten thousand francs if the deal was made. Next the buyer talked about keeping him aboard as captain, someone he could trust.'

Immediately regretting those last words, she glanced at Maigret and seemed grateful to him for not smiling ironically at the idea of someone trusting an ex-con.

Instead, Maigret was thinking things over. Even he was startled by the frank simplicity of her story, which had the troubling ring of truth.

'But you haven't any idea who this buyer is?'

'No.'

'Or where your brother was going to meet him again?'

'No.'

'Or when?'

'Very soon. The refitting was supposed to be done in Norway, he said, and the yacht would leave within a month for the Mediterranean, bound for Egypt.'

'A Frenchman?'

'I don't know.'

'And you were at Notre-Dame-des-Dunes just now to retrieve your shell?'

'Because I thought that, if it were found, everyone would think something completely different from the truth. Admit it: you don't believe me . . .'

Instead of an answer, another question.

'Did you see your brother?'

She shuddered in surprise.

'When?'

'Last night . . . or this morning.'

'Louis is here?'

She seemed frightened, disoriented.

'The *Saint-Michel* has arrived.'

His words appeared to reassure her, as if she had been afraid that her brother had shown up without the schooner.

'So he's on his way to Caen?'

'No, he spent the night aboard one of the dredgers.'

'Let's go – I'm cold . . .'

The wind from the ocean was freshening as the overcast deepened.

'Does he often sleep on an empty old boat?'

When she didn't reply, the conversation died on its own. They walked on, hearing only the sand crunching softly underfoot and the snapping leaps of tiny crustaceans, disturbed at their feast of seaweed swept in by the tide.

Maigret was seeing two images come together in his mind's eye: a yacht . . . and a gold fountain-pen.

Then his thoughts came like clockwork. Earlier that morning, the pen had been difficult to explain because it didn't fit in with the *Saint-Michel* or its rough-and-ready crew.

A yacht . . . and a fountain-pen. That made more sense! A wealthy, middle-aged man is looking for a pleasure yacht and loses a gold pen.

But how to explain why this man, instead of going ashore at the quay, took the schooner's dinghy, hauled himself up the jetty ladder and hid in a waterlogged dredger?

'The night Joris vanished, when your brother came to see you, did he talk about this buyer? He didn't mention, for example, that the man was aboard the *Saint-Michel*?'

'No. He simply said that the deal was almost settled.'

They were approaching the foot of the lighthouse. Joris'

cottage was just to the left, and flowers planted by the captain were still blooming in the garden.

Julie's face fell. She seemed sad and looked around vacantly like someone who no longer knew what to do with her life.

'You'll probably be going to see Joris' lawyer soon, for the reading of the will. You're a wealthy woman, now.'

'Fat chance!' she said curtly.

'What do you mean?'

'You know perfectly well. All this nonsense about a fortune, huh . . . The captain wasn't rich.'

'You don't know that.'

'He didn't keep secrets from me. If he'd had hundreds of thousands of francs, he would have told me. And he wouldn't have hesitated, last winter, to buy himself a two-thousand-franc shotgun! He really wanted that gun . . . He'd had a look at the mayor's and found out how much it cost.'

They had reached the front gate.

'Are you coming in?'

'No. Perhaps I'll see you later.'

She hesitated before going inside the cottage, where she would be all alone.

Nothing much happened over the next few hours. Maigret hung around the dredger like someone with time on his hands and a deep fondness for strange sights. There were chains, capstans, dredging buckets, huge pipes . . .

Towards eleven, he had an aperitif with the bar regulars.

'Has anyone seen Big Louis?'

They had seen him, rather early that morning. He had

73

downed two glasses of rum there and taken off along the main road.

Maigret was drowsy. Perhaps he had caught a chill the night before. In any case, he felt as if he were coming down with the flu and looked it, too. He seemed lethargic.

But it didn't appear to bother him – and that bothered everyone else! His companions stole worried glances at him; the general mood was subdued.

'What should I do with the dinghy?' asked Delcourt.

'Tie it up somewhere.'

Maigret tossed out another disquieting question.

'Has a stranger been seen around here, this morning? Or anything unusual, over by the dredgers?'

No, nothing! But now that he had asked, they all felt something was in the offing.

It was funny: they all expected high drama! A presentiment? The feeling that this chain of events still had one more link to go?

A boat sounded its horn at the lock. The men stood up. Maigret trudged to the post office to see if there were any messages for him. A telegram from Lucas announced his arrival at 2.10.

And when that time came, so did the little train that runs along the canal from Caen to Ouistreham. With its 1850-model carriages, it looked like a child's toy when it appeared in the distance, but it pulled into the station with squealing brakes and a cloud of hissing steam.

Lucas came towards Maigret with his hand out-stretched – and was surprised by the inspector's weary gloom.

'What's wrong?'

'I'm fine.'

Lucas couldn't help laughing at that, even though Maigret was his boss.

'You certainly don't look it! Well, since I haven't had any lunch . . .'

'Come to the hotel, they must still have something there to eat.'

They sat in the main dining room, where the hotel-owner served the sergeant himself. He hovered around Maigret and Lucas as they talked quietly and when he brought over the cheese he saw his chance to speak up.

'Did you hear what happened to the mayor?'

Maigret reacted with such alarm that the man was taken aback.

'Oh, nothing serious! It's just that a little while ago, at home, he fell while coming downstairs. No one knows how he managed to do that, but his face is so battered that he had to take to his bed.'

Then Maigret had a brainwave. That is the right word, for his intellect deciphered the incident in an instant.

'Is Madame Grandmaison still in Ouistreham?'

'No, she took the car and left early this morning with her daughter. I suppose they went to Caen.'

Maigret's flu vanished.

'Are you going to sit there all day?' he grumbled.

'Of course,' replied Lucas placidly, 'it's easy for someone with a full stomach to wax impatient watching a hungry man tuck into his food. Let's say, three minutes more . . . Oh! Don't take the camembert away yet please!'

6. The Fall Down the Stairs

The hotel-owner had not been lying, but the news he had passed on had been somewhat exaggerated, for Monsieur Grandmaison was not laid up in bed.

When Maigret arrived at the Norman villa, after sending Lucas to keep his eye on the dredger, he saw through the picture window a form sitting in the classic pose of the patient who must stay home to convalesce.

Although the inspector could not see his features, it was obviously the mayor.

Further from the window stood another man, but that was all Maigret could determine.

After ringing the bell, he heard more comings and goings inside than were necessary to open a front door. The maid arrived at last, a middle-aged, rather pinch-faced creature who must have felt infinite contempt for all visitors, for she never bothered to unclench her teeth.

Having opened the door, she went back up the few steps leading to the front hall and left Maigret to shut the door himself. Then she knocked on a double door and stood aside as the inspector entered the mayor's study.

There had been something peculiar about that whole performance. Nothing blatantly bizarre, but jarring little things and a slightly uneasy atmosphere.

The house was a large one, almost new, in the prevailing

style of the French seaside, but given the wealth of the Grandmaison family, chief stockholders in the Compagnie Anglo-Normande, a touch more luxury might have been expected. Perhaps they had saved such embellishment for their residence in Caen?

Maigret had hardly entered the room when he heard: 'Here you are, inspector!'

The voice came from over by the window. Monsieur Grandmaison was ensconced in a massive club chair with his legs propped up on another chair. It was difficult to see him, because of the backlighting, but he was clearly wearing a scarf loosely knotted around his throat instead of a stiff collar, and covering the left half of his face with one hand.

'Do sit down.'

Maigret took a tour of the room, then finally went to sit facing the ship-owner. He struggled to repress a smile, for the mayor was quite a sight.

His left cheek, which his hand could not entirely conceal, was puffy, and his upper lip swollen, but what he was most intent on hiding was a stunning black eye.

The man's face wouldn't have seemed that funny if he hadn't been trying so hard to be as dignified as usual in spite of it! He was undaunted and stared at Maigret with frank suspicion.

'You've come to report the results of your inquiry?'

'No. You received me so graciously the other day, with the gentlemen from the public prosecutor's office, that I wished to thank you for your hospitality.'

There was never a hint of irony in Maigret's smiles. On

the contrary! The more mocking he was, the more studiously solemn his face.

He looked around the study again. The walls were full of technical drawings of freighters and photographs of the ships of the Compagnie Anglo-Normande. The furniture was nondescript, good-quality mahogany, but nothing more. On the desk, a few files, some letters, telegrams.

And the inspector seemed to gaze with particular pleasure at the beautifully waxed floor.

'It seems you've had an accident?'

Sighing, the mayor shifted his legs and grumbled, 'A misstep, coming down the stairs.'

'This morning? Madame Grandmaison must have been terrified!'

'My wife had already left.'

'The weather is hardly suitable for a seaside vacation, true! Unless one is an avid duck hunter . . . I suppose that Madame Grandmaison is at Caen with your daughter?'

'Paris, actually.'

The ship-owner was carelessly dressed. Dark trousers, a dressing gown over a grey flannel shirt, felt slippers.

'What was there at the foot of the stairs?'

'What do you mean?'

'What did you land on?'

A venomous look. A strained reply.

'The floor, obviously.'

A lie, a whopper! Falling on the floor never gave anyone a black eye. Still less the marks of fingers tightly wrapped around one's throat!

As it happened, whenever the scarf moved the tiniest

bit, Maigret could easily see the bruises it was intended to conceal from him.

'You were alone in the house, naturally.'

'Why "naturally"?'

'Because such accidents always happen when there's no one around to come and help!'

'The maid was doing her shopping.'

'She's the only servant here?'

'I also have a gardener, but he has gone to Caen. He had some errands there.'

'You must have been in real pain.'

What worried the mayor the most was precisely this solemnity on Maigret's part. He sounded sincerely sympathetic!

Although it was only 3.30, evening was already coming on, and the room was growing dark.

'May I?'

The inspector pulled his pipe from his pocket.

'If you'd like a cigar, there are some on the mantelpiece.'

There was a whole pile of packing-cases in a corner. A bottle of aged Armagnac, on a tray. The tall doors were of varnished pitch pine.

'And what about your investigation?'

Maigret gestured vaguely, making an effort not to look over at the door to the drawing room, a door that was vibrating for some mysterious reason . . .

'Nothing to report?'

'Nothing.'

'Would you like my opinion? It was a mistake to let people think that this was a complicated matter.'

'Evidently!' grunted Maigret. 'As if there were anything

complicated about what happened! One evening, a man disappears and gives no sign of life for well over a month. He's found in Paris six weeks later, with a skilfully repaired bullet wound in his skull, having lost his memory. Brought home, he is poisoned that same night. Meanwhile, three hundred thousand francs have been deposited, from Hamburg, into his bank account. It's simple! Clear as day!'

This time, there was no mistaking the inspector's meaning, despite his genial tone.

'Well, perhaps the matter is less complicated than you think, in any case,' insisted the mayor. 'And supposing that this death truly is mysterious, it would be better, I believe, not to wantonly create an atmosphere of anxiety. By speaking of such things in certain cafés, one ends by unsettling minds that alcohol has already made only too unstable.'

Directing his stern, authoritative gaze at Maigret, he spoke slowly, carefully, as if delivering an indictment.

'And on the other hand, the police have made no effort to obtain information from the proper authorities! Even I, the local mayor, know nothing of what's happening down in the harbour.'

'Does your gardener wear espadrilles?'

The mayor looked immediately at the shining parquet, where footprints were clearly visible on the waxy surface. The pattern of rope-soled shoes was unmistakable.

'I have no idea!'

'Pardon me for interrupting you! A thought that occurred to me . . . You were saying?'

But Monsieur Grandmaison had lost the thread of his speech.

'Would you reach me down that box of cigars? ....
That's it, thank you.'

He lit one, moaning faintly because he was opening his
jaws too wide.

'In short, how far have you got? Surely you've come up
with *some* interesting leads by now.'

'Not really!'

'That's curious, because those people down in the harbour aren't lacking in imagination, in general, and certainly
not after a few aperitifs.'

'I suppose you've sent Madame Grandmaison off to
Paris to spare her the distress of all this drama? And any
unpleasantness that might be still to come?'

They were not fighting out in the open. Yet they were
sparring with a certain covert hostility fuelled simply, perhaps, by the social divide between them.

Maigret drank down at the Buvette de la Marine with
fishermen and lock workers.

The mayor entertained guests from the public prosecutor's office with tea, liqueurs and petits fours.

Maigret was simply a man, impossible to categorize.

Monsieur Grandmaison belonged to a very definite
social milieu. He was the most important man in a small
town, the scion of an old bourgeois family, a prosperous
and respectable ship-owner.

True, he put on democratic airs and cheerfully greeted
the members of his constituency in the streets of Ouistreham. But this was a condescending, electoral democracy!
He was patronizing them.

Maigret looked so rock-solid it was almost frighteningly

impressive. Monsieur Grandmaison, with his pink face and rolls of fat, was fast losing a grip on his authority and sang-froid.

So he waxed indignant to regain the upper hand.

'*Monsieur Maigret,*' he began.

And it was a thing of beauty, the way he said those first two words!

'*Monsieur Maigret* . . . I take the liberty of reminding you that, as mayor of this town—'

So placidly that the mayor could only stare at him, the inspector rose and walked to a door that he opened as casually as you please.

'Do come in, Louis! It's irritating to watch a door that can't stop shaking and to hear you breathing behind it.'

Maigret must have been disappointed if he had hoped to create a dramatic scene: Big Louis did as he was told. He came into the study with his head and shoulders awry, as usual, and stood looking at the floor like both a simple sailor overawed by the villa of a local magnate and a man suddenly finding himself in a difficult stuation.

As for the mayor, he was puffing heavily on his cigar and staring straight ahead.

Daylight was almost gone from the study. A gas lamp outside was already lit.

'May I turn on the light?' asked Maigret.

'Just a minute . . . Close the curtains, first. There's no need for people going by to . . . That's it, the cord on the left, pull it slowly.'

Big Louis remained standing motionless in the middle

of the study. Maigret switched the light on, walked over to the slow-combustion stove and automatically began to poke the fire.

It was a great habit of his. As was the way he would stand in front of a fire with his hands clasped behind him, toasting his back, when he was absorbed in reflection.

Had the situation changed? Be that as it may, there was a glint of mockery in the look Monsieur Grandmaison gave the inspector, who was thinking hard.

'Was Big Louis here when you . . . had your accident?'

'No!'

'Too bad! That's how you might have, for example, in tumbling down the stairs, landed on his bare fist . . .'

'And it would have allowed you to stir up anxiety in the little harbour cafés, by telling fanciful tales. Best wrap this business up, don't you think, inspector? There are two of us . . . We are both working on this case. You come here from Paris . . . You've brought with you Captain Joris, in a pitiful state, and all the evidence indicates that it was not in Ouistreham that he met with such injury . . . You were here when he was killed . . . You go about your inquiry in your own way.'

The man's voice was positively cutting.

'As for me, I have been the mayor here for ten years. I know my constituents. I consider myself responsible for their well-being. As mayor I am also the local chief of police. Well . . .'

When he paused to take a long puff on his cigar, the ash dropped off and crumbled over his dressing gown.

'While you've been patronizing the harbour bistros, I, too, have been busy with this case, if you please!'

'And you summoned Big Louis.'

'As I will summon others if I see fit. And now, I suppose that you have nothing more of importance to tell me?'

He rose, a trifle stiffly, to see his visitor to the door.

'I trust,' murmured Maigret, 'that you will have no objection if Louis comes with me? I already questioned him last night, but there are a few more things I'd like to ask him.'

Monsieur Grandmaison gestured dismissively by way of reply. It was Big Louis who stayed right where he was, staring at the floor as if nailed to it.

'Are you coming?'

'Nah! Not right now.'

It was more grunting than speaking, like everything Julie's brother said.

'Let me point out,' observed the mayor, 'that I have no objection at all to his going with you! I insist that you take note of this, so that you will not accuse me of trying to stymie your investigation. I sent for Big Louis to inquire about certain matters. If he prefers to stay, it's probably because he has something else to tell me.'

All the same, there was tension in the air, and even fear – and not just in the air, for there was almost panic in the mayor's eyes.

And the smile on Big Louis' face was one of brutish satisfaction.

'I'll wait for you outside,' the inspector told him.

But the reply he received was from the mayor.

'It was nice seeing you, Detective Chief Inspector Maigret.'

The inspector left the study. Hurrying from the kitchen, the maid sullenly showed him to the front door without a word and closed it behind him.

The road was deserted. In the window of a house a hundred metres away, Maigret saw a light; there were a few others, but at long intervals, for the villas on the Riva-Bella road are surrounded by extensive gardens.

Hands in his pockets, hunched over, Maigret walked to the front gate and looked out over empty ground, since all that part of Ouistreham runs alongside the dunes. Beyond the gardens lie only sand and beach grass.

A form in the darkness; a voice . . .

'That you, inspector?'

'Lucas?'

They quickly drew together.

'What are you doing here?'

Without taking his eyes from the villa's grounds, the sergeant whispered, 'The man from the dredger . . .'

'He came out?'

'He's here!'

'Has he been here long?'

'Barely fifteen minutes . . . Right behind the house.'

'Came in over the fence?'

'No. It looks as if he's waiting for someone. I heard your footsteps, so I came to check.'

'Show me where.'

They went around the garden to the back of the villa, where Lucas swore softly.

'What's the matter?'

'He's gone.'

'You're sure?'

'He was over by the clump of tamarisks.'

'You think he went inside?'

'No idea.'

'Stay here. No matter what happens.'

Maigret ran back to the road. No one . . . A ray of light showed at the study window, but the sill was out of reach.

He hurried back through the garden to ring at the door. The maid opened it almost immediately.

'I think I left my pipe in the study.'

'I will go and see.'

She left him on the threshold, but as soon as she had gone he went quietly to the study door and peeked in.

The mayor was still in his chair with his legs propped up. A small table had been set next to him. And on the other side of it sat Big Louis.

They were playing draughts.

The ex-con moved a piece and barked, 'Your turn!'

The mayor, looking up in exasperation at the maid still hunting for the pipe, exclaimed, 'You can see for yourself that it's not here! Tell the inspector he must have left it somewhere else. Your move, Louis.'

Perfectly at home, Louis called after her, 'And then bring us something to drink, Marguerite!'

7. Orchestrating Events

When Maigret left the villa, Lucas could tell there was trouble coming. The inspector was ready to explode, with staring eyes that seemed to see nothing.

'Didn't find him?'

'I don't think it's even worth looking for him. We'd need too many men to hunt down someone hiding in the dunes.'

His overcoat buttoned all the way up, Maigret thrust his hands into his pockets and chewed the stem of his pipe.

'See that gap between the curtains?' he said, pointing to the study window. 'And that low wall, right in front? Well, once you're standing on the wall, I think you could see into the room.'

Lucas was almost as big as his boss, but not as tall. He hoisted himself on to the wall with a sigh, checking both ways along the road to make sure no one was coming.

The wind had picked up at sundown, a sea wind that strengthened with each passing minute and shook the trees.

'Anything?'

'I'm not up high enough. Fifteen or twenty centimetres short.'

Maigret walked over to a heap of stones by the road and brought back a few.

'Try these.'

'I can see the edge of the table, but not the people.'

And the inspector went to fetch more stones.

'That does it! . . . They're playing draughts. The maid's bringing them some steaming glasses, must be hot grog.'

'Stay there.'

Maigret began pacing up and down the road. A hundred metres on: the Buvette de la Marine, then the harbour. A baker's van went by. The inspector almost stopped it to make sure no one was hiding inside, but instead he just shrugged.

There are some seemingly simple police operations that prove impracticable. Hunting for the man who had vanished into thin air behind the mayor's villa, for example! A search of the dunes, along the beach, in the harbour and village? Roadblocks everywhere? Twenty policemen would not be enough. And a smart fellow would slip through the net anyway.

Maigret didn't even know who he was or what he looked like.

The inspector returned to the wall, where Lucas was still standing in an awkward position.

'What are they doing?'

'Still playing draughts.'

'Talking?'

'Not a peep. The convict has both elbows on the table and is already on his third grog.'

Fifteen minutes later, something rang inside the house. Lucas called Maigret over.

'Phone call. The mayor's trying to get up . . . but Big Louis got there first.'

Although they couldn't hear the conversation, it seemed to have pleased Big Louis.

'They're done?'

'Back to the draughts.'

'Stay there!'

Maigret went off to the bar. A few of the evening regulars were playing cards and invited the inspector to join them for a drink.

'Thanks, not now. Is there a telephone here, mademoiselle?'

It was on the wall in the kitchen. An old woman was cleaning fish.

'Hello! Ouistreham switchboard? Police! Would you tell me who just called the mayor's villa?'

'Caen, sir.'

'What number?'

'It was 122. That's the train station café.'

'Thank you.'

He left the kitchen and for a good long moment stood lost in thought in the middle of the bar.

Suddenly he murmured, 'It's twelve kilometres from here to Caen . . .'

'Thirteen!' Delcourt informed him, having just walked in. 'And how's it going, inspector?'

Maigret hadn't heard him.

' . . . On a bike, that's barely half an hour . . .'

He remembered that the lock workers, most of whom lived in the village, came down to the harbour on bikes that sat all day right across from the bar.

'Would you mind seeing that none of the bicycles is missing?'

Then Maigret's brain went into gear and moved smoothly through the chain of events.

'Damn! It's my bike that's gone . . .'

Unsurprised, the inspector asked no further questions but returned to the phone in the kitchen.

'Give me the Caen police . . . Yes . . . Thank you . . . Hello! Police headquarters? Detective Chief Inspector Maigret here, Police Judiciaire. Is there still a train for Paris tonight? . . . What's that? . . . Not before eleven? . . . No, but listen, please write this down.

'First, make sure that Madame Grandmaison – the ship-owner's wife, yes! – did in fact leave for Paris in her car.

'Next, find out if any stranger showed up at Grandmaison's office or residence today . . . Yes, that's easy, but there's more. You are taking all this down, right?

'Finally, check all the garages in Caen. How many are there? Around twenty? . . . Then only those renting out cars will be of interest. Start with the ones close to the train station . . . Right! You're looking for someone who rented a car, with or without a driver, for Paris – or who might have bought a second-hand car . . . Hello? Don't hang up, damn it! . . . The man probably abandoned a bicycle in Caen.

'Yes, that's it. But do you have enough officers to take care of all that? . . . Good, that's it then : . . . And as soon as you have any information whatsoever, call me at the Buvette de la Marine in Ouistreham.'

The harbour men at their aperitifs in the overheated main room had heard every word. When Maigret walked back in, their faces were grave, tense with anxiety.

'You think my bike . . . ?' began one lock worker, but in vain.

'A grog!' Maigret called out curtly.

Gone was the fellow who had smilingly raised a glass with them all over the past few days. He hardly saw or recognized them now.

'The *Saint-Michel*, she's not back from Caen?'

'Supposed to be here in time for the evening tide, but with this weather she may not be able to get out.'

'A storm?'

'We're in for some rough weather at least. And the wind's veering to the north, that's not good news. Can't you hear?'

And there was a kind of hammering, from the waves breaking on the jetty pilings. Wind gusts rattled the door.

'If there's a call for me, let me know. I'll be about a hundred metres up the road.'

'Right by the mayor's house?'

Maigret had a terrible time lighting his pipe outside. The massive clouds running low across the sky seemed to snag on the crowns of the poplars lining the road. From five metres away, he couldn't make out Lucas standing on his wall.

'Anything?'

'They've stopped playing draughts. All of a sudden Louis just swept the pieces off the board as if he were tired of the game.'

'What are they doing?'

'The mayor's slumped in his chair. The other one's smoking cigars and drinking grogs. He's already picked a dozen cigars to pieces, with a sarcastic look on his face, as if to provoke Grandmaison on purpose.'

'How many grogs?'

'Five or six.'

Maigret couldn't see anything but that thin strip of light down the façade. Some builders going home after work pedalled past towards the village. Next came a farmer's cart. Sensing a human presence in the darkness, the driver whipped up his horse and looked back nervously a few times.

'The maid?'

'Haven't seen her. She must be in her kitchen. Will I be up here much longer? Because in that case, you'd best get me more stones, so I don't have to stand on tiptoe.'

Maigret brought some. The din of the ocean was growing louder. All along the beach, the waves must have been almost two metres high, crashing into white foam on the sand.

Down by the harbour, a door opened and closed. It was the bar. A figure appeared, trying to see in the darkness, and Maigret ran over to him.

'Ah! It's you. You're wanted on the phone.'

Caen was calling back already.

'Hello? Detective Chief Inspector? How did you know! . . . Madame Grandmaison went through Caen this morning, heading for Paris. She left at noon, in a car. Her daughter stayed at home in the care of the governess. And regarding the stranger, you were right. At the very first garage we checked, the one across from the station, we learned that a man had arrived by bicycle and wanted to rent a car, no driver. They told him that the garage did not arrange that sort of thing.

'The man seemed impatient and asked if he could at least buy a car in a hurry, second-hand if possible, so they sold him one for twenty thousand francs, which he paid, cash on the barrel. It's a yellow touring car, bearing the letter W because it was for sale.'

'Do they know which way he went?'

'The man asked for directions for the road to Paris through Lisieux and Évreux.'

'Telephone the national and local police in Lisieux, Évreux, Mantes and Saint-Germain. Warn Paris that all the entrances to the city must be watched, especially Porte Maillot.'

'We're to stop the car?'

'And arrest its occupant, yes! Do you have a description?'

'From the garage-owner . . . A rather tall man, middle-aged, in an elegant, light-coloured suit.'

'Same instructions as before: phone me at Ouistreham as soon as—'

'Excuse me, sir: it's almost seven o'clock, and the Ouistreham exchange shuts down at seven. Unless you go to the mayor's house . . .'

'Why is that?'

'Because the phone number there is 1 and is directly linked at night to Caen.'

'Send someone to the post office. If any call coming through their telephone exchange asks for the mayor, listen in on the conversation. Do you have a car?'

'Yes, a small one.'

'That will be enough to come and alert me. At the Buvette de la Marine, as before.'

Back in the main room, Captain Delcourt was bold enough to ask, 'Is it the murderer you're after?'

'I've no idea!'

The men there could not understand how Maigret, so cordial and friendly until then, could now be so distant and even cantankerous. He left without telling them anything. Outside, he plunged again into the roar of the wind and the sea and had to button his overcoat up tightly, especially to cross the bridge, which was shaking in the storm.

Standing in front of Joris' cottage, he hesitated for a moment, then looked through the keyhole. He saw the kitchen door, its glass panels lit up. Behind them a form went back and forth between the stove and the table.

He rang. Julie froze, holding a dish, then set it down, opened the door and came into the front hall.

'Who is it?' she asked anxiously.

'Inspector Maigret!'

She opened the door and stood aside. She was nervous. Her eyes were still red and she kept glancing fearfully around her.

'Come in, I'm glad you're here. If you knew how scared I am, by myself in this house! I don't think I'll be staying on.'

The inspector entered the kitchen, which was as clean and neat as always. On the white oilcloth covering the table sat only a small bowl and some bread and butter. A pot on the stove was giving off a sweet aroma.

'Hot chocolate?' exclaimed the inspector, surprised.

'I haven't any heart to cook just for myself . . . So I made some chocolate.'

'Pretend I'm not here. Go on, eat . . .'

She fussed a bit, then did fill her bowl and added big pieces of buttered bread to soak. Staring straight ahead, she ate this with a spoon.

'Your brother hasn't come to see you yet?'

'No! I don't understand . . . I went as far as the harbour, just now, hoping to see him. When they're at loose ends, sailors always hang around the harbour.'

'Did you know your brother was a friend of the mayor?'

She looked at him as if in shock.

'What do you mean?'

'They're busy playing draughts together.'

She thought he was joking and, when persuaded that he was not, she became frightened.

'I don't understand . . .'

'Why?'

'Because the mayor keeps his distance from people . . . And he certainly does not like Louis. He's tried to make trouble for him a few times. He didn't even want to let him live here.'

'And with Captain Joris?'

'What about him?'

'Was Monsieur Grandmaison friends with the captain?'

'The way he is with everyone! A handshake in passing. He makes a little joke. A remark about the weather. But that's all. Sometimes, I already told you this, he would take the captain along hunting . . . although that was simply so he wouldn't be alone.'

'Have you received a letter from the lawyer yet?'

'Yes! It says I'm the sole legatee. What exactly does that mean? Is it true that I'll inherit the house?'

'Along with three hundred thousand francs, yes!'

She calmly kept eating, then shook her head and murmured, 'That's impossible . . . It makes no sense. I've told you, I'm certain the captain never had three hundred thousand francs!'

'Where did he sit? Did he eat in the kitchen?'

'Where you are, in the wicker armchair.'

'Did you eat together?'

'Yes . . . Except that I would get up to do my cooking and handle the plates. He liked to read his paper while he ate . . . Once in a while he'd read an article out loud.'

Maigret was not in a mood for sentiment. And yet, something about the restful atmosphere was getting to him. The clock seemed to tick more slowly than clocks anywhere else. The long reflection from the brass pendulum swung back and forth on the wall in front of him. And the sweet smell of the chocolate . . . The wicker of the armchair creaked familiarly at his slightest movement, as it must have when Captain Joris was sitting in it.

Julie was afraid, off in the cottage on her own. And yet she was loath to leave it! Maigret realized that there was something keeping her in this snug and comfortable place.

Julie rose and went to the door. He watched her. She let in the white cat, which went over to a dish of milk at the foot of the stove.

'Poor Puss!' she said. 'Her master was fond of her . . .

96

After dinner, Puss would sit on his lap until he went to bed.'

A calm so intense that it became in some way threatening! A warm, heavy calm . . .

'Do you really have nothing to tell me, Julie?'

She looked up at him questioningly.

'I believe I'm about to discover the truth. A word from you might help me . . . That's why I'm asking you if you have anything else to say.'

'I swear to you . . .'

'About Captain Joris?'

'Nothing!'

'About your brother?'

'Nothing, I swear.'

'About anyone who came here whom you didn't know!'

'I don't understand . . .'

She kept eating that sugary mush, the mere sight of which nauseated the inspector.

'Well, I'd best be going.'

She seemed disappointed; she would be alone again. She was anxious to ask him one last question.

'Tell me, about the funeral . . . I suppose they can't go on waiting much longer? A dead person . . . I mean . . .'

'He's on ice,' said Maigret reluctantly.

And a great shiver ran through her.

'Are you there, Lucas?'

It was pitch black, impossible to see anything now. And the roar of the storm drowned out everything else. In the harbour, each man at his post awaited the arrival of a boat from Glasgow that had missed the channel and could be heard whistling out between the jetties.

'I'm here.'

'What are they doing?'

'Eating. I wish I were. Some shrimp, clams, an omelette and what looks like cold veal.'

'At the same table?'

'Yes. Big Louis is still leaning on his elbows.'

'Talking?'

'Not much. Every now and then their lips move, but they must not be saying much.'

'Drinking?'

'Louis, yes! There are two bottles of wine on the table. Nice old bottles. The mayor keeps filling Louis' glass.'

'Trying to make him drunk?'

'Right. The maid's face is something to see. Whenever she has to go behind the sailor, she gives him a wide berth.'

'No more phone calls?'

'No. Now here's Louis blowing his nose in his napkin and standing up. Wait. He's fetching a cigar. The box is on the mantelpiece. He's holding it out to the mayor, who's shaking his head. The maid's bringing in the cheese.'

'If I could just sit down!' added Sergeant Lucas plaintively. 'My feet are ice-cold. I'm afraid to move for fear I might tumble off . . .'

It wasn't enough to impress Maigret, who had been in similar situations at least a hundred times.

'I'll bring you something to eat and drink.'

The inspector's place was set at his table in the Hôtel de l'Univers. Without sitting down, he simply devoured a piece of pâté and some bread. He then made a sandwich for his colleague and carried off the rest of the bottle of Bordeaux.

'And here I've prepared a bouillabaisse for you the likes of which you'd not find even in Marseilles!' wailed the hotel-owner.

But nothing could touch the inspector, who returned to the wall to ask the same question for the tenth time.

'What are they doing?'

'The maid has cleared the table. The ship-owner, in his armchair, is chain-smoking. I do believe Louis is falling asleep. He still has his cigar between his teeth, but I don't see the slightest wisp of smoke.'

'Did he have any more to drink?'

'A full glass of the bottle that was on the mantelpiece.'

'Armagnac,' muttered Maigret.

'Hold on! There's a light upstairs . . . It must be the maid going to sleep. The mayor is standing up. He—'

The sound of voices over by the bar. A car engine. Some faint words . . .

'A hundred metres on? In the house?'

'No, outside.'

Maigret set out to intercept the car, which was heading his way. He saw the uniformed men inside and stopped it some distance from the villa so as not to alert the mayor.

'Any news?'

'Évreux has informed us that the man in the yellow car has been arrested.'

'Who is it?'

'Well, listen – he's protesting the arrest! He threatens to inform his ambassador.'

'He's a foreigner?'

'Norwegian! Évreux gave us the name over the phone, but it was impossible to understand. Martineau, or Motineau . . . His papers seem to be in order, and the police want to know what they should do.'

'Have them bring him here, with the yellow car. They must have an officer who can drive. Hurry, get back to Caen and try to find out where Madame Grandmaison stays when she goes to Paris.'

'They already told us that a little while ago, it's the Hôtel de Lutèce, Boulevard Raspail.'

'Telephone from Caen to find out if she arrived and what she's doing. Wait! If she is there, phone the Police Judiciaire for me and ask them to have her discreetly followed by an inspector.'

The car needed to back up at three different angles to turn around on the narrow road. Maigret went back once again to Lucas on his wall but found him clambering down.

'What are you doing?'

'There's nothing more to see.'

'They've left?'

'No, but the mayor came over to the curtains and drew them tightly closed.'

A hundred metres away, the boat from Glasgow moved gently into the lock as orders were given in English. A sudden gust carried the inspector's hat off in that direction.

The topmost light in the villa suddenly went out, leaving the façade in complete darkness.

8. The Mayor's Inquiry

Maigret was standing in the middle of the road, both hands in his pockets, frowning.

'Something worrying you?' asked Lucas, who knew his boss.

'Inside is where we should be,' grumbled the inspector, studying the villa's windows one after the other.

But they were all closed tight. There was no way to get into the house. Maigret went quietly up to the front door, leaned down and listened, gesturing to Lucas for silence. In the end they both had their ears glued to the oak panel.

They heard no voices, could identify no words. There were footsteps in the study, however, and some steady, dull thuds.

Were the two men fighting? Unlikely, for the pounding was too evenly spaced. Two struggling men would come and go, staggering and bumping into furniture, with pauses and flurries of punches. This was like a pile-driver. And they could even distinguish the rhythmic breathing of the man landing the blows: 'Huh! . . . Huh! . . . Huh! . . .'

In counterpoint, low moaning.

The two policemen looked at each other. The inspector turned towards the lock and pointed; the sergeant understood and pulled a set of skeleton keys from his pocket.

'Don't make any noise,' whispered Maigret.

The house seemed silent now. Ominously quiet. No more blows. No more footsteps. Maybe – but this was hard to tell – the hoarse gasping of an exhausted man.

Lucas signalled. The door opened. Dim light filtered into the hall from around the study door on the left. Maigret shrugged with irritation and anger. He was exceeding his authority – by a considerable extent, even, and in the home of a hostile official like the mayor of Ouistreham.

'Too bad!'

From the hall he could clearly hear breathing, but only one person's. No movement. Lucas had his hand on his revolver. Maigret opened the door with one shove.

He stopped short, as stunned and confused as he had ever been. Had he been expecting to catch someone red-handed?

This was something else! And completely baffling. Monsieur Grandmaison's lip was split, his chin and dressing gown all bloodied, his hair mussed up, and he looked as punch-drunk as a boxer who had stumbled to his feet after a knock-out.

And he seemed barely able to stand, propped up against a corner of the mantelpiece but leaning so far back that it seemed impossible for him to stay upright.

A few steps away, a rough-looking Big Louis with blood on his still-clenched fists. The mayor's blood!

It was Big Louis' panting they had heard out in the corridor. He was the one out of breath, doubtless from beating the other man. He smelled of alcohol. The glasses on the small table had been tipped over.

The policemen were so astounded and the others so

exhausted that it was a good minute at least before anyone said a word.

Then Monsieur Grandmaison wiped his lip and chin with a corner of his dressing gown and stammered, while trying to stand up straight, 'What the . . . What . . . ?'

'Do excuse me,' said Maigret courteously, 'for having entered your home unannounced. I heard a noise, and the front door was not locked.'

'That's not true!'

The mayor had evidently recovered his spirits.

'In any case, I'm glad we arrived in time to protect you and . . .'

He glanced over at Big Louis, who did not seem the least bit upset and was now even smiling strangely while studying the mayor's reaction.

'I do not need to be protected.'

'But this man has attacked you . . .'

Standing at a mirror, Monsieur Grandmaison was trying to make himself more presentable and seemed frustrated at failing to stop his lip from bleeding.

It was an extraordinary and unsettling display of strength and weakness, self-assurance and cowardice.

With his impressive shiner, wounds and bruises, his face had lost its slightly childish, rosy-cheeked glow, and there was a dull look in his eyes.

He was recovering his aplomb surprisingly quickly, though, and, leaning against the mantelpiece, he soon challenged the policemen.

'I take it that you broke into my house.'

'Pardon me: we wished to come to your rescue.'

'Not true, because you did not know that I was in any danger at all! *And ... I ... was ... not!*'

Maigret studied the impressive figure of Big Louis from head to toe.

'Nonetheless, I trust that you will allow me to take this gentleman away.'

'Absolutely not!'

'He beat you. And rather brutally at that.'

'We've sorted it all out! And it's nobody's business but my own!'

'I have every reason to believe that it was on him that you fell this morning, while going a bit quickly downstairs.'

Big Louis' grin was as pretty as a picture. He was in heaven. While he was getting his breath back, he missed nothing of what was happening and found these developments delightful. He, at least, must have understood all the hidden facets of the situation and could savour the jest to the full!

'I did tell you earlier today, Monsieur Maigret, that I'd undertaken my own investigation. I am not meddling with yours. Do me the favour of not interfering with mine. And don't be surprised if I file a complaint against you for illegal entry.'

It was hard to tell whether he cut a tragic or comic figure. He was standing on his dignity and drawing himself up imposingly – with a bleeding lip! And a face that was one big bruise! And a dressing gown in tatters!

Big Louis even seemed to be egging him on.

The main thing was what had just happened, and it

wasn't hard to picture: the ex-convict, punching so hard and so much and so well that he wore himself out.

'Please forgive me if I don't leave right away, Monsieur Grandmaison. Given that you are the only person in Ouist-reham with a telephone connection at night, I've taken the liberty of having a few calls directed here.'

The mayor's only response was, 'Shut the door!' – for it had been left wide open.

Then he picked up one of the cigars lying scattered on the mantelpiece and tried to light it, but its contact with his lip must have been painful, for he threw it violently away.

'Lucas, would you get Caen on the line for me?'

Maigret kept studying the mayor, then Big Louis, then the mayor again. And he was having difficulty marshalling his thoughts.

For example, a first impression might suggest that, of the two opponents, it was Monsieur Grandmaison who was the underdog, the weakest not only physically but morally.

He had been beaten, discovered in the most humiliating circumstances.

Well, not at all! Within a few minutes he had recouped his sang-froid and some of his bourgeois respectability.

He was almost calm. His look, haughty.

Big Louis had the easy part. He had been the winner. He was neither wounded nor even bruised. Moments before, his blissful smile had evoked an almost childlike joy. And now he was the one beginning to look uneasy, unsure of what to do, where to go, even where to look.

So Maigret wondered . . . Assuming that one of these

two was the boss, which was it? He just didn't know. Grandmaison, at times; Louis, at others.

'Hello? Caen, Police Headquarters? . . . Detective Chief Inspector Maigret asked me to tell you that he will be at the mayor's house all night . . . Yes . . . That's telephone number 1 . . . Hello! Do you have any news? Lisieux already? . . . Thanks . . . Yes.'

Turning to Maigret, Lucas announced, 'The car just went through Lisieux. It'll be here very soon.'

'I believe I heard you say—'

'That I would spend the entire night here, yes. With your permission, of course. Twice, now, you have mentioned the inquiry you have personally undertaken, and I believe the best thing would be for you to authorize me to pool the information we have both gathered on our own.'

Maigret was not being sarcastic. He was furious. Furious at the unbelievable situation in which he had landed himself. Furious at being flummoxed by the case.

'Would you explain to me, Big Louis, why, when we arrived, you were busily . . . um . . . punching the daylights out of the town mayor?'

But Big Louis said nothing, looking at the mayor himself as if to say, 'You, speak up!'

'That is my affair,' remarked Monsieur Grandmaison crisply.

'Of course! Everyone has the right to have himself beaten up if he likes that!' grumbled Maigret. 'Lucas, get me the Hôtel de Lutèce.'

The shot hit home. Monsieur Grandmaison's hand

tightened its grip on the marble mantelpiece. He opened his mouth to speak.

Lucas was talking on the phone.

'A three-minute wait? . . . Thank you . . . Yes.'

'Don't you find that this inquiry is taking an odd turn?' asked Maigret. 'By the way, Monsieur Grandmaison, perhaps you can be of help here. As a ship-owner, you must know people from many countries. Have you heard of a certain . . . just a moment . . . a certain Martineau . . . or Motineau . . . from Bergen or Trondheim . . . A Norwegian, in any case?'

Silence! Big Louis' eyes had gone hard. He reached automatically for one of the glasses lying on the table and poured himself a drink.

'Well, it's too bad you don't know him. He's on his way here.'

That was it. Not worth adding a single word. They wouldn't answer. They wouldn't even flinch. It was obvious from the poses they had taken.

In a change of tactics, Monsieur Grandmaison, still leaning against the mantelpiece, was contemplating the floor with studied indifference while he toasted his calves before the fire of coal briquettes.

But what a face! Slack features, splotched with blue and red, bruises and a bloody chin! A mixture of focused energy and panic, or distress.

Big Louis? He had parked himself astride a chair. After yawning three or four times, he seemed to be dozing.

The phone rang. Maigret grabbed the receiver.

'Hello? The Hôtel de Lutèce? . . . Don't cut me off: I'd like to speak to Madame Grandmaison . . . Yes! She should have arrived this afternoon or this evening . . . Yes, I'll wait.'

'I assume,' said the mayor in a flat voice, 'that you have no intention of involving my wife in your . . . rather bizarre actions at this moment?'

No reply. Maigret waited, the receiver at his ear, staring at the tablecloth.

'Hello, yes! . . . Repeat that? . . . She has already left? . . . One moment . . . From the beginning. When did the lady arrive? . . . Seven o'clock, fine . . . With her car and driver . . . You say she dined at the hotel, then was summoned to the telephone . . . She left directly afterwards? . . . Thank you . . . No! . . . That's enough.'

No one faltered. Monsieur Grandmaison seemed calmer. Maigret hung up, then picked up the receiver again.

'Hello! Caen central? Police here. Would you tell me if anyone at this number put through a call to Paris today at any time before this present call? . . . Yes? . . . About fifteen minutes ago? . . . The Hôtel de Lutèce, wasn't it? . . . Thank you.'

Beads of perspiration stood out on Maigret's forehead. He slowly filled a pipe with little taps of his index finger. Then he poured himself a drink, using a glass from the table.

'I suppose you realize, inspector, that everything you're doing now is illegal. You broke into my house. You're staying here without my permission. You might very well cause great upset to my family and, finally, you are treating me like a criminal in the presence of a third person. You will pay for all this.'

'Understood!'

'Since I am no longer master in my own house, either, I would like permission to go to bed.'

'No!'

Maigret caught the sound of a car in the distance.

'Go and wait for them at the door, Lucas.'

He tossed a shovelful of coal into the fireplace out of habit and turned around at the very moment when the new arrivals entered: two policemen from Évreux flanking a man in handcuffs.

'Leave us,' he told the escorts. 'Wait for me outside, even if it takes all night.'

The mayor had not budged. Neither had the sailor. You would have thought that they hadn't seen a thing, or didn't want to. As for the newcomer, he was relaxed, and a smile hovered about his lips when he noticed Monsieur Grand-maison's swollen face.

'Who is in charge here?' he asked, glancing around.

Maigret, raising his shoulders as if in surprise at the policemen's effrontery, pulled a small key from his pocket and removed the handcuffs.

'Thank you. I was rather astonished at—'

'At what?' thundered Maigret angrily. 'At being arrested? Are you sure you were really all that astonished?'

'That's to say, I'm still waiting to learn what I'm supposed to have done.'

'Let's start with stealing a bicycle!'

'Correction! Borrowed! The garage-owner from whom I bought the car will tell you that! I left him with the bicycle and instructions to send it back to Ouistreham with some monetary compensation for its owner.'

'Really! . . . But, you don't actually seem to be Norwegian . . .'

The man neither looked nor sounded Norwegian. He was tall, well built, still young. His nicely tailored clothes were a bit the worse for wear.

'Excuse me! I am Norwegian, perhaps not by birth, but I've been naturalized.'

'And you live in Bergen?'

'Tromsø, near the Lofoten islands.'

'Are you a businessman?'

'I own a factory for processing waste products from cod-fishing.'

'Including, for example, salted cod's roe.'

'The roe and other things. With the heads and livers we make oil. With the bones, fertilizer.'

'Perfect! That's just perfect! Now all I need to know is what you were doing in Ouistreham on the night of the 16th of September.'

Without turning a hair, the man looked slowly around and said, 'I was not in Ouistreham.'

'Where were you?'

'And where were you? What I mean is,' he said with a smile, 'would you be able, out of the blue, to say what you were doing at a given hour on a given day after more than a month had gone by?'

'Were you in Norway?'

'Probably.'

'Look.'

And Maigret held out to him the gold fountain-pen, which the Norwegian put in his pocket as calmly as you please.

'Thank you.'

He was a really good-looking man, the mayor's age and height, but slimmer, yet muscular. His dark eyes were intensely alive. And the smile on his thin lips betrayed his immense self-confidence.

Politely, pleasantly, he answered the inspector's questions.

'I rather feel there must be some mistake, and I'd very much like to continue on my way to Paris.'

'That's a different matter. Where did you first meet Big Louis?'

Maigret was disappointed: the man's eyes did not flick over to the sailor.

'Big Louis?' he repeated.

'You met Joris during his voyages as a merchant ship captain?'

'Sorry, I don't understand.'

'Evidently! And if I ask you why you preferred to sleep aboard a laid-up dredger instead of in a hotel you'll look at me with big round eyes . . .'

'Certainly. Well, put yourself in my place.'

'Yet you arrived yesterday in Ouistreham on the *Saint-Michel*. You came ashore in the dinghy before she entered the harbour. You holed up in the dredger and spent the night there. This afternoon, you walked around this very villa, then . . . borrowed a bicycle and sped off to Caen. Purchased a car. Left for Paris. Is it Madame Grandmaison you were going to join at the Hôtel de Lutèce? If so, don't bother to continue your journey. Unless I'm much mistaken, she'll arrive here later tonight.'

Silence. The mayor had become a statue, and his stare was so vacant that it seemed devoid of life. Big Louis was scratching his head and yawning, still astride his chair, with everyone else standing around him.

'So your name is Martineau?'

'Jean Martineau, yes.'

'Well, Monsieur Jean Martineau, why don't you think things over? Consider whether you might not have something to tell me after all. The chances are good that someone here in this room will one day be committed for trial.'

'Not only have I nothing to say to you, but I would like permission to contact my consul so that he may take the usual steps . . .'

That made two of them! Grandmaison had threatened to file a complaint; Martineau was going to follow suit. Only Big Louis wasn't trying to warn him off, instead reacting philosophically to whatever happened, as long as there was something to drink.

Outside the tempest was raging and, at high tide, it had reached its full strength.

What Lucas thought showed in his face: 'Now we're in hot water! Either we come up with something, or we're cooked.'

Maigret was tramping up and down the room, puffing ferociously at his pipe.

'So neither of you knows anything about Captain Joris' disappearance or his death?'

Grandmaison and Martineau shook their heads. Silence. Maigret kept looking over at Martineau.

Then, hurried footsteps outside; a nervous rapping at the front door. After a moment's hesitation, Lucas went to open it. Someone ran in: Julie, all out of breath, who gasped, 'Inspector . . . My . . . My brother . . .'

And she was struck dumb at the sight of Big Louis, who stood up, dwarfing her with his great size.

'Your brother?' Maigret prompted her.

'Nothing . . . I . . .'

She tried to smile as she caught her breath but, retreating backwards, she bumped into Martineau.

'Sorry, monsieur,' she stammered, without seeming to recognize him.

The wind roared in through the forgotten front door, left wide open.

9. The Conspiracy of Silence

Julie was explaining why she had come, in short, hesitant sentences.

'I was alone in the house . . . I was frightened. . . . I'd gone to bed with all my clothes on . . . Someone started pounding on the door . . . It was Lannec, my brother's skipper.'

'The *Saint-Michel* is in?'

'She was in the lock when I passed by. Lannec wanted to see my brother right away . . . Seems they're in a hurry to set out. I told him Louis hadn't even come to visit! And the skipper's the one who got me worried, muttering things I didn't understand . . .'

'Why did you come here?' asked Maigret.

'I asked Lannec, was Louis in any danger – and he told me yes, that maybe it was already too late . . . So I asked around in the harbour, and they told me you were here.'

Big Louis was staring at the floor, looking irritated. He shrugged, as if to indicate that women get all worked up about nothing.

'You're in danger?' asked Maigret, trying to meet his eyes.

Big Louis laughed. A great booming noise, much more simple-minded than his usual laughter.

'Why was Lannec worried?'

'Now how would I know?'

'In short,' said Maigret pensively, looking around at everyone, 'you don't know anything. None of you do!' he added, with an edge of bitterness. 'You, Monsieur Grandmaison, you've never met Monsieur Martineau and don't know why Big Louis – who makes himself at home in your house, playing draughts with you and eating at your table – would suddenly begin punching your face into pudding.'

Not a word.

'What am I saying? You seem to find this perfectly natural! You don't defend yourself! You won't file a complaint! You won't even throw Big Louis out of your house.'

He turned to Big Louis.

'You, you haven't a clue either! You sleep aboard the dredger but have no idea who else is with you there. You repay the hospitality of this house by using the master of it as a punchbag. You have never seen Monsieur Martineau in your life . . .'

Not a flicker of response. Everyone was stubbornly studying the carpet.

'And you, Monsieur Martineau, you're just the same. Do you even know how you got from Norway to France? No! You'd rather sleep in a bunk in the abandoned dredger than in a hotel bed. You take off on a bike, buy a car to drive to Paris. But you know nothing. You've never met Monsieur Grandmaison, Big Louis, or Captain Joris. And of course you, Julie, know even less than the others.'

Discouraged, he looked over at Lucas. His sergeant understood. They couldn't arrest them *all* . . . Every single one of them was guilty of inexplicable behaviour, lying or conflicting statements.

But not one thing that would stand up in court!

It was eleven o'clock. Maigret knocked out his pipe in the fireplace.

'I must ask you all,' he intoned grumpily, 'to remain at the disposal of the judicial authorities . . . I will certainly have occasion to question you further, in spite of your ignorance. I take it, Mayor Grandmaison, that you have no intention of leaving Ouistreham?'

'No.'

'Thank you. Monsieur Martineau, you could take a room at the Hôtel de l'Univers, where I am staying.'

The Norwegian bowed slightly.

'Accompany Monsieur Martineau to the hotel, Lucas.'

He turned to Julie and Big Louis.

'You two, come with me.'

Once outside, Maigret dismissed the two policemen waiting for him there, then watched Lucas and Martineau set off immediately for the hotel, where the proprietor was waiting up for his guests.

Julie had rushed from the cottage without her coat, and her brother, seeing her shivering, made her put on his jacket.

The storm made talking too difficult. They had to walk bent over with the wind constantly whistling in their ears and chilling their faces so badly that their eyelids hurt.

The bar in the harbour was lit up, full of lock workers who were dashing in, between vessels, to get warm and down hot grogs. Their faces turned towards the trio, who plodded on through the gale, over the bridge.

'Is that the *Saint-Michel*?' asked Maigret.

A schooner was leaving the lock, making for the outer harbour, but he thought it seemed much taller than the one he remembered.

'She's in ballast,' grunted Louis.

Meaning that the *Saint-Michel* had unloaded in Caen and was travelling empty to pick up a fresh cargo.

Just as they were coming to Joris' cottage, a shadowy figure approached them. They had to peer into his face to recognize him. The man spoke shakily to Big Louis.

'There y'are at last. Hurry, let's get under way!'

Maigret looked hard at the little Breton skipper, then at the waves attacking the jetties in an endless roar. The sky was a startling panorama of furious, roiling clouds.

The *Saint-Michel*, moored to a piling in the darkness, showed only one tiny light from a lamp on the deckhouse.

'You mean to go out in this?'

'Of course!'

'Where to?'

'La Rochelle, for a cargo of wine.'

'You absolutely must have Big Louis?'

'You really think just two could manage her in this blow?'

Standing there listening, stamping her feet, Julie was cold. Her brother kept looking back and forth between Maigret and the *Saint-Michel*, her rigging creaking in the storm.

'Go and wait for me aboard!' Maigret told the skipper.

'But we . . .'

'But what?'

'Tide's on the ebb, we've got only two hours left.'

There was something in his eyes . . . He was clearly uneasy, apprehensive, kept shifting from one foot to the other and couldn't look at anything for more than a second or two.

'Me, I've got my living to earn!'

Maigret caught an exchange of glances between the skipper and his mate. There are moments when intuition goes into high gear, and Maigret was sure he had read the little captain right: 'Boat's not far, only one line to cast off; a single swing at this police fellow and we're away . . .'

'Go and wait for me aboard!' repeated Maigret.

'But . . .'

The inspector signalled to the two others to follow him inside.

Maigret was seeing the brother and sister alone together for the first time. They were all three in Captain Joris' kitchen, where a good fire was drawing so well in the iron stove that the purring flames would sometimes snap and crackle.

'How about something to drink?' said the inspector to Julie, who fetched a carafe of spirits and some matching glasses with painted flowers on them.

He was in the way, he could tell. Julie would dearly have liked to be alone with Big Louis, who watched her attentively with what was clearly great affection and a kind of brutish tenderness.

Like the consummate housekeeper she was, Julie did not sit down after serving the two men but restoked her fire.

'To the memory of Captain Joris,' said Maigret, raising his glass.

There was a long silence. This suited the inspector. He wanted everyone to have time to absorb the warm, quiet atmosphere of the kitchen.

The steady humming of the fire gradually joined with the tick-tock of the pendulum clock into a kind of music. Safe from the chilly winds outside, their cheeks grew pink, and their eyes shone brightly. And the pungent aroma of calvados perfumed the air.

'Captain Joris,' said Maigret softly. 'Here I am, sitting at his place, in his armchair . . . A wicker chair that creaks with every move I make. If he were alive, he'd be coming in from the harbour and probably asking for another glass, to warm himself up. Right, Julie?'

She looked at him, wide-eyed, then turned away.

'He wouldn't go right up to bed. I bet he'd take off his shoes . . . You'd fetch him his slippers . . . He'd say, "Dirty weather – but the *Saint-Michel* still insisted on heading out to sea, may God keep her!"'

'How did you know?'

'What?'

'That he used to say, "May God keep her"? That's it, exactly . . .'

She was deeply moved, and there was a touch of gratitude in the look she gave Maigret.

Big Louis hunched over a little more.

'Well, he won't ever say it again. Too bad! He was a happy man. He had a pretty little house, a garden full of flowers he loved, his savings . . . Everyone really liked him, it seems. And yet there was someone who put an end to all that, suddenly, with a sprinkling of white powder in a glass of water.'

Julie's face seemed to collapse. She fought hard to hold back her tears.

'A pinch of white powder and it's all over! And whoever did it will probably be happy, he will, because no one knows who he is! He was doubtless just with us a little while ago . . .'

'Be quiet!' begged Julie with clasped hands, and the tears finally streamed down her face.

But the inspector knew where he was going. He kept speaking in a low voice, slowly, giving each word its due. And there wasn't much play-acting in it, for he was caught up in the mood himself. He too felt the nostalgia of that atmosphere in which he conjured up the sturdy form of the late harbourmaster.

'Dead, he has only one friend left . . . Me! A lone man who is fighting to find out the truth, to prevent Joris' murderer from living happily ever after . . .'

Overwhelmed by her sorrow, Julie was sobbing as Maigret went on.

'The thing is, everyone around the dead man keeps silent, everyone lies, as if everyone had some reason to feel guilty, as if they were all accomplices in what happened!'

'That's not true!' wailed Julie.

Big Louis, growing more and more uncomfortable, poured himself more calvados and refilled the inspector's glass.

'Big Louis, first of all, remains silent.'

Julie looked at her brother through her tears, as if struck by the true meaning of those words.

'He knows something,' continued Maigret. 'He knows many things. Is he afraid of the murderer? . . . Is he in danger in some way?'

'Louis!' cried his sister.

And Louis looked away, with a face made of stone.

'Say it isn't true, Louis! . . . Won't you listen to me?'

'Don't know what the inspector . . .'

He just couldn't remain still any longer. He got to his feet.

'Louis is the biggest liar of the bunch! He claims not to know the Norwegian but he does! He claims not to have any dealing with the mayor, and I find him in the man's house, beating him to a pulp . . .'

That vague smile appeared on the ex-convict's lips. But Julie wasn't mollified.

'Oh, Louis! Is that true?'

When he didn't answer, she clutched at his arm.

'Then why don't you tell the truth? You haven't done anything, I know you haven't!'

He pulled away, but looked torn . . . Perhaps he was weakening. Maigret didn't give him time to pull himself together.

'Just one tiny truth, a single scrap of information in this whole mess of lies would probably be enough to untangle everything!'

But, no. In spite of his sister's pleading looks, Louis shook himself like a giant harassed by furious little enemies.

'I don't know anything.'

'Why won't you talk?' said Julie sternly, already growing suspicious.

'I don't know anything!'

'The inspector says—'

'I don't know anything!'

'Listen, Louis . . . I've always believed in you, you know that. And I defended you, even to Captain Joris . . .'

Flushed with regret over that last remark, she quickly went on.

'You must tell the truth. I can't take this any more. And I won't stay any longer in this house, by myself.'

'Stop talking, Julie,' sighed her brother.

'What do you want him to tell you, inspector?'

'Two things. First, who Martineau is. Then, why the mayor let himself be beaten up.'

'You hear that, Louis? . . . It's not so bad!'

'I don't know anything.'

Now she was getting angry.

'Louis, listen to me! I'm going to end up thinking that . . .'

And the fire kept on purring. And the ticking of the clock was slow, stretching the reflected lamplight along on its copper pendulum.

Louis was too tall, too strong, too rough, with his lopsided head and shoulder, for that tidy little cottage kitchen. He didn't know what to do with his big callused hands. His shifty eyes could find no place to rest.

'You must speak!'

'I got nothing to say.'

He tried to pour himself another drink, but she pounced on the carafe.

'That's enough! There's no point in you getting any drunker.'

She was painfully anxious. She had the confused feeling that real tragedy was at stake, at that very moment. She clung to her hope that one word might make everything clear.

'Louis, that man, that Norwegian . . . He's the one who was supposed to buy the *Saint-Michel* and become your boss, isn't he?'

'No!' barked Louis.

'Then who is he? We've never seen him around here. And foreigners don't come here off-season . . .'

'I don't know.'

Julie kept at him, with a subtle feminine instinct.

'The mayor always hated you. Did you really eat supper at his house tonight?'

'That's true.'

She was almost dancing with impatience.

'But then, tell me something! You must! Or I swear I'll start believing that . . .'

She couldn't go on. She was wretched. She looked around at the wicker armchair, the familiar stove, the clock, the carafe with its painted flowers.

'You were fond of the captain, I know it! You said so a hundred times, and if you two fell out it's because . . .'

But now she had to explain all that.

'Don't go thinking the wrong thing here, inspector! My brother was fond of Captain Joris, and the captain liked him as well, it's just that there was . . . But nothing serious! Louis goes a little wild when he's got money in his pocket and then he spends it all, any old which way . . . The captain knew that he used to come here to wheedle my savings out of me. So he lectured him . . . That's all! If he ended by forbidding him to come here, it was for that, so that he wouldn't go off with any more of my money! But he'd tell me that Louis was really a good fellow at heart, whose only fault was that he was weak.'

'And Louis,' said Maigret slowly, 'might have known that, with Joris dead, you would inherit three hundred thousand francs!'

It happened so quickly that the inspector almost got the worst of it. As Julie uttered a piercing scream, Big Louis leaped with all his strength at Maigret, trying to get his hands around his throat.

The inspector managed to grab one of his wrists on the fly, and with slow but steady pressure, he twisted the sailor's arm behind his back, growling, 'Hands off!'

Julie wept even more piteously, her elbows up against the wall, her head buried in her crossed arms.

'My God,' she moaned faintly, 'my God . . .'

'Don't you want to talk, Louis?' said Maigret sternly, releasing his grip on him.

'I have nothing to say.'

'And if I arrest you?'

'So what!'

'Follow me.'

Julie cried out:

'Inspector! I'm begging you! For the love of God, Louis, talk to him!'

They were already at the kitchen door. Big Louis turned around, his face red, his eyes glittering. His expression was beyond words. He reached with one hand for his sister's shoulder.

'My Lilie, I swear to you . . .'

'Don't touch me!'

He hesitated, took a step towards the front hall, then turned again.

'Listen . . .'

'No! No, get out!'

So he followed Maigret, dragging his feet. Stopping at the threshold, he was tempted to look back . . . but did not. The front door closed behind them. They had not taken five steps into the storm when the door flew open on the young woman's pale form.

'Louis!'

Too late. The two men walked straight ahead, into the night.

A gust of rain soaked them in a matter of seconds. They couldn't see a thing, not even the edges of the lock. A voice hailed them, though, rising up through the darkness.

'That you, Louis?'

It was Lannec, aboard the *Saint-Michel*. He had heard their footsteps and stuck his head up through the hatchway. He must have known that his first mate was not alone, for he then spoke rapidly in Low Breton, saying, 'Jump on to the fo'c'sle and we'll head out.'

Maigret, who had understood, now waited, unable to find the true outline of the *Saint-Michel* in the pitch dark. All he could see of his companion was a wavering mass of a man, his shoulders gleaming in the rain.

10. *The Three Men of the* Saint-Michel

A glance at the black hole of the ocean; a more furtive one at Maigret. With a shrug, Big Louis grunted to the inspector, 'You coming aboard?'

Maigret now saw that Lannec held something in his hand: the end of a mooring line. Tracing it with his eyes, he saw that it passed once around a bollard and went back aboard. In other words, the *Saint-Michel* had been made fast in a way that allowed the skipper to cast off without putting a man ashore.

The inspector said nothing. He knew the harbour was deserted. Julie was doubtless sobbing in her kitchen 300 metres away, and there was no one else nearby but the people sheltering in the warmth of the Buvette de la Marine.

He stepped on to the bulwarks handrail and jumped down to the deck, followed by Louis. Even protected by the jetties, there was rough water in the outer harbour, and the *Saint-Michel* rose on each wave as if on a man's heaving chest.

Nothing in the darkness but yellow glints on wet things. On the fo'c'sle, a vague form: the captain, looking at Louis in astonishment. He wore tall rubber boots, an oilskin slicker, a sou'wester, and he was still clutching the mooring line.

No one did anything. They all waited . . . The three men of the *Saint-Michel* must have been studying Maigret, who cut such a strange figure with his velvet-collared overcoat and bowler hat, held clamped to his head to preserve it from the gale.

'You will not leave tonight!' he announced.

No protest. But a look passed between Lannec and Louis that meant, 'We sail anyway?' . . . 'Better not.'

The wind was now so violent that they could barely stand upright, and again it was Maigret who took the lead by going to the hatchway, which he remembered from his first visit.

'We'll talk – and bring that other sailor down too!'

He did not want anyone left up on deck, out of his sight. The four men went down the hatch.

Off came boots and oilskins. The gimballed lamp was lit, and there were glasses on the table next to a greasy sea-chart heavily marked with pencil lines.

Lannec put two coal briquettes into the small stove but looked askance at Maigret and seemed hesitant to offer him a drink. As for old Célestin, he went to huddle in a corner, peevish and uneasy, wondering why he had been brought down to the cabin.

Everyone's attitude clearly meant the same thing: no one wanted to speak up, because no one knew how matters stood. The puzzled skipper stared at Louis, who looked back at him helplessly.

What he had to say would require such long, complicated explanations!

'You've thought it over?' muttered Lannec hoarsely, after coughing to clear his throat a little.

Maigret was sitting on a bench, elbows on the table,

playing absently with an empty glass so smudged that it was now opaque.

Standing there, Big Louis had to bow his head to avoid touching the roof.

Lannec fiddled around in the cupboard to give himself something to do.

'Thought what over?'

'I don't know which legal powers you have. What I do know is, I answer only to the maritime authorities. They alone can stop a vessel from entering or leaving a port.'

'Meaning?'

'You're keeping me from leaving Ouistreham. I've got cargo to take on in La Rochelle, plus there's penalties to pay for every day I'm late.'

They were getting off on the wrong foot, with this serious, semi-official approach. Maigret knew that game by heart! Hadn't the mayor threatened him almost in the same way? And hadn't Martineau then talked of appealing, not to the maritime authorities, but to his consul?

He paused a moment to take a deep breath and give them all a rapid – and now strangely cheerful – glance.

'Why don't you give all that a rest!' he said in Breton. 'And pour us a drink instead.'

It was a long shot. The old sailor was the first one to turn towards Maigret in amazement. Big Louis' face relaxed.

'You're a Breton?' asked Lannec, still wary.

'Not quite. I'm from the Loire, but I studied for some time in Nantes.'

What a look! The face coastal Bretons make at the

mention of inland Bretons, and especially the halfway Bretons around Nantes.

'Any of that Dutch gin left from the other day?'

Lannec brought the bottle and slowly filled the glasses, happy to have something to do. Because he still didn't know what to do about Maigret. There he was: big, affable, pipe between his teeth, his bowler pushed back on his head, settling in nicely.

'You can sit down, Big Louis.'

The first mate obeyed. The uneasy atmosphere still lingered some, but in another way. The sailors felt awkward, not being able to return the inspector's cordiality, but they had to remain on their guard.

'Your health, boys! And admit it: by keeping you here tonight I'm saving you from a nasty run.'

'It's the harbour channel, mostly,' murmured Lannec. A swallow of gin, and then, 'Once we're out of the gat, we're clear . . . But with that current from the Orne, and all those sandbanks, the channel's tough. Every year she grounds some ships.'

'The *Saint-Michel*'s never had real trouble?'

The captain quickly touched wood. Célestin growled angrily at the mere mention of bad luck.

'The *Saint-Michel*?' exclaimed Lannec. 'She's maybe the best schooner on the coast. Listen! Two years ago, in dense fog, she fetched up on the rocky English coast in a hell of a surf. Any ship but her would have left her bones there. Well! She floats away on the next tide, didn't even need to lie up in dry dock.'

Maigret felt they could get along fine in this vein, but

he wasn't in the mood to talk ships all night. Their wet clothes were beginning to steam. Water was snaking down the ladder. And the ever-increasing heaving of the ship, which slammed now and then into the pilings, was beginning to tell on the inspector.

'She'll make a fine yacht!' he exclaimed, looking off into the distance.

So that was it! Lannec flinched.

'Yes, she'd make a fine one,' he countered. 'With only the deck to change. And a little less canvas, especially aloft.'

'Has the Norwegian signed the contract?'

Lannec looked sharply at Louis, who sighed. They would have given a great deal, those two, to talk privately for even a few seconds. What had Louis already revealed? What could the captain safely say?

Big Louis was wearing his stubborn look. He knew the fix they were in but had no way of explaining what was going on to the skipper. It was too complicated!

And would all end badly, of course. He had best have a drink. He poured himself one, drank it straight off and faced the inspector. He wasn't even really feeling up for a fight, but simply resigned.

'What Norwegian?'

'Well, the Norwegian who isn't exactly a Norwegian. Martineau. Anyway, it certainly wasn't in Tromsø that he saw the *Saint-Michel*, since she never went that far north.'

'Mind you, she could! Could handle all the way to Archangel, right enough.'

'When's he taking delivery?'

The old sailor snorted derisively, off in his corner. His contempt was not directed at Maigret, but at the three men of the *Saint-Michel*, himself included.

'I don't know what you mean,' replied Lannec lamely.

Maigret elbowed him gaily in the ribs.

'Come off it! Really, boys. Stop looking as if you were all at a funeral! And wipe those grumpy looks off your pig-headed Breton faces . . . Martineau promised to buy the schooner, but has he actually purchased it?'

Inspiration struck.

'Show me the muster roll.'

He felt that shot strike home.

'I've no idea where it . . .'

'I told you to give that stuff a rest, Lannec! Show me the crew list, damn it all!'

He was playing the pretend bully, the good-hearted brute. The skipper went to the cupboard for a well-worn briefcase, grey with age. It was full of official documents and business letters from ship-brokers' firms. One thing was new, a big yellow folder containing some impressively large pages: it was the muster roll. It had been drawn up and dated only a month and a half before, on 11 September. Five days before Captain Joris disappeared.

Schooner *Saint-Michel*, 270 gross tons, licensed for the coastal trade. Owner of record: Louis Legrand, Port-en-Bessin. Captain: Yves Lannec. Seaman: Célestin Grolet.

Big Louis poured himself another. Lannec hung his head in embarrassment.

'Look at this! You're the present owner of this boat, Big Louis?'

No reply. Off in his corner, old Célestin bit off a great chunk of his chewing tobacco.

'Listen, boys. There's no point in wasting time over this. I'm not a complete fool, eh? Granted, I'm no expert on life at sea, but Big Louis is flat broke. A boat like this one is worth at least a hundred and fifty thousand francs.'

'I'd never have sold her for that!' Lannec shot back.

'Let's say two hundred thousand. So Big Louis bought the *Saint-Michel* on someone else's behalf! And let's say . . . on behalf of Jean Martineau. For some reason or other, the Norwegian doesn't want anyone to know he owns the schooner . . . cheers!'

Célestin shrugged, as if deeply disgusted by the entire business.

'Was Martineau in Fécamp on the 11th of September, when the sale took place?'

The others just frowned. Louis picked Célestin's quid up from the table and bit off his own chunk of tobacco while the deck-hand spattered the cabin floor with great spurts of brown spittle.

There was a lull in the conversation because the wick of the lamp was charring for lack of fuel. Lannec had to fetch more from the can on deck and returned soaked through. The others sat for a minute in darkness, and when the lamp was relit none of them had moved.

'Martineau was there, I'm sure of it! The boat was purchased in Big Louis' name, and Lannec was to stay aboard, perhaps permanently, perhaps only for a while.'

'For a while . . .'

'Right! I thought so. Long enough to captain the *Saint-Michel* on a most unusual voyage.'

Lannec got to his feet in such agitation that he chewed through his cigarette.

'You came to Ouistreham. On the night of the 16th, the schooner was moored in the outer harbour, ready to head out to sea. Where was Martineau?'

The captain sat down again, still distressed but determined to keep silent.

'On the morning of the 17th, the *Saint-Michel* sails. Who is aboard? Is Martineau still there? Is Joris there too?'

Maigret did not seem like a judge or even a police officer. His voice was still pleasant; there was a glint of mischief in his eyes. It was as if he were playing a game of riddles with his companions.

'You sail to England. Then you set a course for Holland. Is that where Joris and Martineau leave you? Because they have further to go. I have good reasons to believe they go all the way up to Norway.'

Big Louis grunted at that.

'What did you say?'

'That you'll never get anywhere.'

'Was Joris already wounded when he came aboard? Was he injured during your voyage, or only up in Scandinavia?'

He no longer waited for replies.

'All three of you continue your business as usual. You stick close to the northern coast. You're waiting for a letter or telegram informing you of a rendezvous. Last week, you were in Fécamp, the port where Martineau met you the first time. Big Louis learns that Captain Joris has been found in Paris, in a bad way, and will be brought home to Ouistreham. He travels here by train. There is no one in the captain's cottage. He leaves a note for his sister. He returns to Fécamp.'

Maigret sighed, took his time lighting his pipe.

'And here we are! Getting close to the end. You return with Martineau and set him ashore at the entrance to the harbour, which proves he did not want to be seen. Big Louis joins him on the dredger . . . cheers!'

He poured his own drink and drained his glass under the mournful gaze of the three men.

'In a nutshell, the only thing left in order to make sense of everything is to discover why Big Louis went to the mayor's house while Martineau was speeding off to Paris. A bizarre mission: thumping silly a man with the reputation of not suffering common folk lightly.'

Big Louis couldn't help grinning angelically at the memory of his punching sessions.

'There you have it, my friends! Now, try to get it through your skulls that the whole truth will come out in the end. The sooner the better, don't you think?'

And Maigret knocked out his pipe against his shoe, refilled it and started all over.

Célestin had fallen deeply asleep. He was snoring, open-mouthed. Big Louis, his head tipped to one side, was looking at the dirty floor, while Lannec tried in vain to catch his eye and solicit some advice.

At last the captain muttered, 'We have nothing to say.'

There was a noise up on deck. As if a rather heavy object

had fallen. Maigret started; Big Louis stuck his head out of the hatchway, leaving nothing to see except his legs on the ladder.

If he had disappeared up on to the deck, the inspector would no doubt have followed him. There was nothing to hear besides the hammering of the rain and some creaking blocks.

This pause lasted for half a minute, no more. Big Louis came back down, his hair plastered to his forehead by the rain streaming down his cheeks, but at first offered no explanation.

'What was it?'

'A pulley block.'

'How . . . ?'

'Banged into the bulwarks.'

The captain replenished the stove. Did he believe what Louis had just said? In any case, instead of responding to his pleading looks, Louis was shaking Célestin.

'Go and rig the mizzen sheet . . .'

The old man rubbed his eyes, still drowsy. The order was repeated twice more. Then he donned his oilskins and sou'wester and climbed the ladder, stiff with the comfort of recent sleep and angry at being sent out into the cold and rain. He wore clogs that clattered up and down the deck, over their heads.

Big Louis poured himself what was at least his sixth glass, yet he showed no signs of intoxication.

His face was always the same: uneven, a trifle bloated, with big eyes that almost bulged from his head. He seemed to be a man plodding glumly through life.

'What do you think, Louis?'

'About what?'

'Idiot! Have you thought about the fix you're in? Don't you understand that you're the one who'll get it in the neck? Your record, first of all. An ex-convict! Then this schooner you now own even though you haven't a sou to your name. Joris barred you from his house because you'd sponged off him too often! The *Saint-Michel*, here in Ouistreham the evening he vanished. You were here the day he was poisoned . . . And your sister then inherits three hundred thousand francs!'

Did Big Louis have a single thought in his head? His eyes were as vacant as could be. China-doll eyes, staring absently at the wall.

'What's he doing up there?' asked Lannec anxiously, looking over at the half-open hatch. Rainwater was pooling on the floor.

Maigret had not had a lot to drink, albeit enough to bring the blood to his head, especially in that stuffy cabin. And enough to inspire a moment of reverie.

Now that he knew the three men, he could imagine their lives in the world of the *Saint-Michel*.

The one man in his bunk, fully dressed most of the time. Always a bottle and some dirty glasses on the table. At least one man on deck; the comings and goings of his clogs or boots . . . Then that dull, steady sound of the sea . . . The compass in the binnacle with its tiny light . . . The other lamp, swaying up on the mizzen-mast . . .

Eyes peering into the darkness, hunting for the firefly gleam of the lighthouse . . . And the loading docks . . .

Two or three days with nothing to do, spending hours in bistros that are everywhere the same . . .

Strange noises were heard overhead. Was Big Louis also sinking into a deep slumber? A small alarm-clock showed it was already three o'clock. The bottle was almost gone . . .

Lannec yawned, felt around in his pockets for some cigarettes.

Hadn't the ship's company spent the night this way, in this same hothouse atmosphere smelling of close quarters and coal tar, on the day Captain Joris had disappeared? And had the captain been among them then, drinking, struggling against drowsiness?

This time, voices were heard on deck, although the tempest reduced them to a whisper down in the cabin.

Maigret stood up with a frown, saw Lannec pouring himself another drink, saw Big Louis' chin touching his chest and his eyes half closed.

He felt for the revolver in his pocket and climbed the almost vertical ladder.

The hatchway was exactly big enough for a man, and the inspector was much taller and bulkier than the average sailor.

So he couldn't even fight back! Hardly had his head emerged from the hatchway when a gag was placed over his mouth and tied behind his neck.

That was the work of the men on deck, Célestin and someone else.

Meanwhile, down below, the revolver was torn from his right hand and his wrists were bound behind him.

He kicked violently back with his foot and hit something that felt to him like a face, but an instant later a rope coiled around his legs.

'Heave ho!' said the flat, indifferent voice of Big Louis.

That was the hard part. He was heavy. He was pushed from below; pulled from above.

The rain was coming down like a waterfall. The wind was blasting up the channel with unbelievable force.

He thought he saw four silhouettes, but the ship's lantern had been put out, and the passage from warmth and light to freezing night had bewildered his senses.

'One . . . Two . . . And away!'

They swung him over like a sack. He sailed fairly high and landed on the wet stones of the quay.

Louis went over after him and bent down to make sure all his bonds were tight. For a moment the inspector had the ex-convict's face quite close to his and had the impression the man was reluctantly carrying out a sad duty.

'You got to tell my sister . . .' he began.

Tell her what? Louis himself didn't know. Aboard the *Saint-Michel* there were hasty footsteps, creaking, grinding sounds, muttered orders. The jibs were unfurled. The mainsail rose slowly up the mast.

'Remember, you must tell her, I'll see her again one day . . . And maybe you, too.'

He jumped heavily back on deck. Maigret was lying facing out to sea. A lantern on a halyard ran up to the masthead. There was a black figure by the tiller.

'Cast off!'

The mooring rope snaked off the bollards, hauled in

from the boat. The jibs snapped in the wind for an instant or two . . . The bow paid off, and the schooner almost swung completely around, so ferociously was she attacked by the storm.

But no – a heave on the tiller brought her into the wind's eye. She hesitated, seeking her way and, heeling over, shot suddenly between the jetties.

A black mass in the blackness. A tiny dot of light on the deck. Another, on high, at the masthead, already seemed like a star wandering lost in a whirlwind sky.

Maigret could not move. He lay inert, in a puddle, at the edge of infinite space.

Out there, wouldn't they buck themselves up by polishing off that bottle? A few more briquettes would go into the fire.

One man at the tiller; the others in the damp bunks.

Perhaps there was one salty drop among the pearly ones streaming down the inspector's face.

A big, powerful man, in the prime of life, perhaps the most dignified and manly officer of the Police Judiciare, abandoned there until dawn, at the end of a harbour quay, next to a bollard.

Had he been able to turn around, he would have seen the small wooden awning of the Buvette de la Marine, now closed for the night.

11. *The Black Cow Shoal*

The sea was draining away fast. Maigret heard the surf at the end of the breakwaters at first, then further out as the sand of the beach was laid bare.

With the ebb tide, the wind eased, as almost always happens. The piercing rain lost some of its sting. By the time the lowest-lying clouds were paling at the approach of day, the deluges of the night had become a light but even more chilling rain.

Objects were gradually emerging from their inky shrouds. The slanting masts of fishing boats now stranded at low tide stuck up above the mudflats of the outer harbour.

Off inland, the distant lowing of a cow. The church bell ringing gently, discreetly, to announce the low mass at seven o'clock.

But he would have to wait a while longer. Any church-goers would not be passing through the harbour. The lock workers would have no business there before high tide. Only a fisherman, perhaps, might show up . . . But did fishermen bother getting out of bed in such weather?

Maigret, now a sodden heap, thought about all the beds in Ouistreham, the sturdy wooden beds with their enormous down quilts, beds where everyone was snuggling lazily in the warmth of their covers, peeking out resentfully at the blanching window panes and granting themselves a tiny respite before sticking their bare feet down on the floor.

Was Sergeant Lucas in bed, too? No! Because in that case, what had just happened was inexplicable.

The inspector had reconstructed those events this way: Jean Martineau had somehow managed to get rid of Lucas. Why not by tying him up, as he had with Maigret himself? The Norwegian then went straight to the *Saint-Michel*, where, hearing Maigret's voice, he waited patiently for someone to appear. Then Big Louis stuck his head out the hatch. Martineau whispered instructions to him or showed him a note he had written.

The rest was simple. There had been that noise up on deck. Louis sent Célestin up from the cabin. Martineau and the old sailor talked, luring Maigret up to investigate.

And when he was halfway there, the team on deck silenced him while those below immobilized his arms and legs.

By now the schooner must have been well outside the three-mile limit for territorial waters. Unless she were to put in at a French port, which wasn't likely, Maigret had no way to intercept her.

Maigret kept still. He had noticed that every time he moved, a little water crept in under his overcoat.

He had one ear on the ground and began identifying the successive sounds he heard. He recognized the noise of the pump in Joris' garden: Julie was up! She must have been out in her clogs, pumping water for her morning ablutions. But she would not come into town. Day hadn't properly dawned yet, so her kitchen light would be on.

Footsteps . . . A man was crossing the bridge . . . Stepping on to the stone wall . . . Walking slowly . . . He threw something that sounded like a bundle of ropes from the top of the quay into a dinghy.

A fisherman? Maigret struggled to change his position and saw the man, twenty metres away, about to go down the iron jetty ladder to the water. In spite of his gag, he managed to make muffled cries.

Looking around, the fisherman spied the black heap and stared at it suspiciously for a long time. At last he made up his mind to draw closer.

'What're you doing there?'

And having vaguely remembered what precautions to take at a crime scene, he added cautiously, 'Mebbe I'd best go fetch the police first.'

He did remove the gag, however. The inspector negotiated with him, and the man, still somewhat dubious, began to untie the bonds, muttering curses at whoever had tied such knots.

The waitress over at the bar was just opening the shutters. Even though the wind had fallen, the sea was still running high, but the waves were no longer thundering in as they had during the night. There were massive swells that rose up over the sandbanks to crest at least three metres and more in waves that crashed in a dull boom, as if the whole continent were being shaken.

The fisherman was a little old man with a bushy beard who remained leery of the situation but unsure of what to do.

'The local police still need to know . . .'

'But I keep telling you: I am a kind of plain-clothes police officer!'

'A plain-clothes police officer,' repeated the old fellow hesitantly.

The old salt's eyes turned naturally to the sea, swept along the horizon, stopped at a point to the right of the jetties, off towards Le Havre, then fixed their appalled gaze on Maigret.

'What's the matter with you?'

The man was too upset to reply, and Maigret only understood why after looking out to sea himself.

The bay at Ouistreham was almost completely high and dry. The sand, the colour of ripe wheat, stretched out for more than a mile, to the purling, pure white surf.

And to the right of the jetty, not more than a kilometre away, was a vessel stranded half on the sand, half in the water, which was attacking the hull like a battering ram.

Two masts, one of them bearing a square lantern. A Paimpol schooner. It was the *Saint-Michel*.

In that direction, sky and sea were indistinguishable, an expanse of greyish-white.

Nothing else there but the black hulk of the beached ship.

'Must've tried leaving too late after the tide turned,' murmured the stunned fisherman.

'Does that happen often?'

'At times . . . Not water enough in the gat! And that Orne current drove her on to Black Cow shoal.'

There was a silent sense of desolation, made even more

forlorn by the drizzle in the air. Seeing the schooner almost completely beached, however, it was hard to imagine that her company had been in any real danger.

When she had set out, though, the sea had still been breaking at the foot of the dunes, adding at least ten battle lines of massive swells.

'Got to tell the harbourmaster . . .'

A small detail. The old man turned automatically towards Joris' cottage, then mumbled, 'Except that . . .'

And he walked off in the opposite direction. The wreck had been spotted by others, now, perhaps from the church porch, for Captain Delcourt arrived looking as if he had dressed in a hurry, followed by three other men.

Delcourt shook hands distractedly with Maigret without noticing that the inspector was rather wet.

'I told them!'

'They'd let you know they were leaving?'

'Well, it's just that when I saw them tie up down here, I had the feeling they wouldn't wait for the next tide. I warned the skipper to watch out for that current.'

Everyone was walking out on to the beach. The wet sand made it heavy going, and there were pools of water thirty centimetres deep. It was a long slog.

'Are the crew in danger?' asked Maigret.

'I doubt they're still aboard. Otherwise, they'd have hoisted the distress flag, tried to signal for help . . . But, wait a minute,' he exclaimed, suddenly uneasy. 'They didn't have their dinghy along! You remember? When the steamer brought it in, we kept it in the dock.'

'So?'

'So they must have had to swim to shore . . . Or . . .'

Delcourt was worried. Certain things bothered him.

'I'm surprised they didn't prop her up, keep her from heeling over . . . Unless she went right over when she grounded on the shoal. But still . . .'

They approached the *Saint-Michel*, and she was a sorry sight. They could see her keel, thick with green underwater paint, and the barnacles encrusting her hull. Sailors were already examining the schooner for any damage, but finding none.

'An ordinary grounding.'

'Nothing serious?'

'It means that at the next tide a tug will probably get her out of there. But what I don't understand is . . .'

'What don't you understand?'

'Why they abandoned her! It's not like them to cut and run. They know the schooner's rock-solid. Look how stoutly she's made! . . . Hey! Jean-Baptiste! Fetch me a ladder!'

The tilting hull still put the bulwark rail more than six metres above the sand.

'No need!'

A snapped shroud was hanging down. Jean-Baptiste used it to clamber up the ship's side like a monkey, then swing over the deck and drop down to it. A few minutes later, he lowered a ladder.

'No one aboard?'

'Not a soul.'

Several kilometres further along the coast they could see the houses of Dives, factory chimneys, then Cabourg and Houlgate, not quite as clearly, and the rocky point concealing Deauville and Trouville.

Maigret climbed up the ladder out of a sense of duty, but he felt unpleasantly dizzy on the sloping deck. An anxious vertigo worse than if the ship had been tossing on a furious sea!

In the cabin, broken glass on the floor, the cupboard doors hanging open . . .

And the harbourmaster didn't know what he should do about all this. He was not the captain of the ship! Should he take responsibility for refloating her and send to Trouville for a tug to heave her off?

'If she goes through another tide she'll be kindling!' he muttered.

'Well, then, do everything possible to save her. You can say that I'm the one who decided . . .'

There was a mournful sense of foreboding in the quiet scene. All eyes kept turning towards the deserted dunes as if expecting to see the *Saint-Michel*'s crew.

Men and children were coming out from the village now. When Maigret returned to the harbour, Julie ran up to him.

'Is it true? Have they been wrecked?'

'No. They ran aground. A strong young man like your brother will surely have pulled through.'

'Where is he?'

The whole affair was ominous, disturbing. The owner of the Hôtel de l'Univers came out to hail Maigret.

'Your two friends haven't come down yet. Should I wake them?'

'Don't bother.'

The inspector went upstairs himself to Lucas' room and found his sergeant almost as tightly bound as Maigret had been.

'There's an explanation . . .'

'Don't need one! Come on.'

'Something's happened? You're all wet . . . And you look exhausted.'

Maigret took him along to the post office, at the highest spot in the village, opposite the church. People were standing out on their doorsteps. Those who could go were dashing down to the beach.

'No chance to defend yourself?' asked Maigret.

'We were going upstairs, and that's where he jumped me. He was behind me, then suddenly pulled my legs out from under me, and the rest was so fast I couldn't fight back. Have you seen him?'

Maigret was causing quite a stir for he appeared to have spent the night up to his neck in water. He couldn't even write his messages in the post office. He was soaking the paper.

'Take the pen, Lucas. Telegrams to all the police stations and town halls in the district: Dives, Cabourg, Houlgate. Those on this side as well: Luc-sur-Mer, Lion . . . Check the map: include even the smallest villages up to ten kilometres inland.

'Four descriptions: Big Louis; Martineau; Captain Lannec; the old sailor answering to the name of Célestin.

'After you've sent the telegrams, call the closest local places, that'll save us some time.'

He left Lucas dealing with his phone and wire assignments.

In a bistro across from the post office, he gulped down a steaming grog while some kids outside pressed their noses to the windows, trying to get a look at him.

Ouistreham was awake now, a nervous, worried village that gazed or hurried towards the sea. And news was travelling . . . Distorted, exaggerated news.

Out on the road, Maigret ran into the old fisherman who had freed him at daybreak.

'You didn't say anything about . . .'

'I said that I found you,' replied the man with indifference.

The inspector gave him twenty francs and returned to the hotel to change. He was shivering all over, felt both hot and cold. He had a bristly growth of beard and great circles under his eyes.

In spite of his fatigue, though, his brain was at work. Even more than usual. He managed to notice everything around him, to question and answer people without losing his train of thought.

When he returned to the post office, it was almost nine o'clock. Lucas was just completing his list of phone calls. The telegrams had already been sent. In reply to his questions, every police station was reporting no sign yet of the four wanted men.

'Monsieur Grandmaison hasn't made any calls, mademoiselle?'

'One hour ago. To Paris.'

She gave him the number. He looked in the phone book: a boys' school, the Collège Stanislas.

'Does the mayor often call that number?'

'Rather often. I think it's his son's boarding school.'

'It's true, he does have a son . . . Of about fifteen, yes?'

'I believe, but I've never seen him.'

'Has Monsieur Grandmaison called Caen?'

'It was Caen that called him. Someone in his family or one of his employees, because the call came from his house there.'

The telegraph was clicking. A message for the harbour-master: 'Tug Athos arriving noon. Signed: Trouville Harbourmaster's Office.'

And the Caen police phoned in at last.

'Madame Grandmaison arrived in Caen at four in the morning. She slept at her home in the Rue du Four. She has just left by car for Ouistreham.'

When Maigret looked out at the beach from the harbour, the sea had retreated so far that the stranded boat was about halfway between the water and the dunes. Captain Delcourt was morose. Everyone was watching the horizon with dread.

Because there could be no mistake. The wind had fallen with the tide, but the storm would return with a vengeance around noon, when the tide turned. That much was clear from the unhealthy grey colour of the sky and the treacherous green of the waves.

'Has anyone seen the mayor?'

'He had his maid inform me that he is ill,' replied Delcourt, 'and that he's leaving me in charge of the rescue operation.'

Maigret headed wearily towards the villa with his hands in his pockets. He rang. It was almost ten minutes before the door opened.

The maid tried to speak but he did not listen, walking into the front hall with such a determined expression that she decided simply to hurry ahead to the study door.

'It's the inspector!' she cried.

Maigret entered the room he was beginning to know so well, tossed his hat on to a chair, nodded to the man stretched out in his armchair.

The bruises of the previous day were much more visible, having turned from red to blue. An enormous coal fire was burning in the fireplace.

One look told Maigret that the mayor intended to say nothing and even to ignore his visitor.

Maigret did the same. He removed his overcoat and went to stand with his back to the fire, like a man intent only on warming himself. The flames felt good on his calves. He smoked his pipe in short, hurried puffs.

'Before the day is over, this whole affair will be resolved!' he finally said, as if musing to himself.

The other man made an effort not to react. He even picked up a newspaper lying within reach and pretended to read it.

'We might, for example, be obliged to go to Caen together.'

'To Caen?'

Monsieur Grandmaison had looked up with a frown.

'To Caen, yes! I should have told you earlier, which would have spared Madame Grandmaison the trouble of coming here for nothing.'

'I don't see what my wife—'

'Has to do with all this!' broke in Maigret. 'Neither do I!'

And he went over to the desk for some matches to relight his pipe.

'It isn't important anyway,' he continued in a lighter tone, 'since it'll all be cleared up soon. By the way, do you know who the current owner of the *Saint-Michel* is, which Delcourt will be attempting to refloat? . . . Big Louis! Except that he's obviously a straw man, acting on behalf of a certain Martineau.'

The mayor was trying to see where Maigret was going with this, but had no intention of talking or – above all – asking him any questions.

'You'll see the chain of events here. Big Louis buys the *Saint-Michel* as a cat's paw for this Martineau five days before Captain Joris disappeared. The schooner is the only boat that left Ouistreham soon after that disappeance, and she went on to England and Holland before returning to France. From Holland, there must be coasters of the same type making regular runs to Norway . . . Martineau happens to be Norwegian. And before turning up in Paris, with a cracked and repaired skull, Captain Joris went to Norway.'

The mayor was listening closely.

'That isn't all. Martineau returns to Fécamp to rejoin the *Saint-Michel*. Big Louis, who is his factotum, is here a few hours before Joris' death. The *Saint-Michel* arrives a little later, with Martineau. And last night, he tries to make a run for it, taking with him most of the men I asked to remain at the disposal of the judicial authorities . . . Except you!'

Maigret paused, and sighed.

'What's still unclear is why Martineau returned and tried to reach Paris, and why you telephoned your wife to have her rush back here.'

'I hope you're not insinuating . . .'

'Me? Not a bit. Listen! There's a car coming. I bet it's Madame Grandmaison arriving from Caen. Would you do me the favour of not telling her anything?'

The doorbell. The maid's footsteps in the hall. The sounds of low voices in conversation, then the maid's face looking in through the half-open door. But why wasn't she saying anything? Why such anxious looks at the master of the house?

'Well?' said he, impatiently.

'It's just that . . .'

Maigret pushed her aside and saw no one in the hall but the uniformed chauffeur.

'You've lost Madame Grandmaison en route?' he demanded bluntly.

'Well . . . Well, she . . .'

'Where did she get out of the car?'

'At the crossroads linking Caen and Deauville. She did not feel well.'

In his study, the mayor was on his feet, breathing heavily. The look on his face was grim.

'Wait for me!' he shouted to the chauffeur.

And finding his way blocked by Maigret's massive form, he hesitated.

'I suppose you're ready to confess . . .'

'Everything. You're right. *We* must go there together.'

12. The Unfinished Letter

The car stopped at a bare crossroads. The chauffeur looked back over his shoulder for instructions. Ever since leaving Ouistreham, Monsieur Grandmaison had not been the same man.

On his home ground he had always managed to control himself, trying to maintain his dignity even under the most distressing circumstances.

Not any more! He was now in a state close to panic, which his battered face made even more obvious. His restless gaze roamed constantly around the passing countryside.

When the car stopped, he looked at Maigret expectantly, but the inspector simply asked, with quiet mischief, 'What shall we do now?'

Not a soul on the road or in the orchards nearby. Madame Grandmaison had clearly not left her car intending to sit down by the roadside. If she had sent her chauffeur on, after alighting there, it was because she was meeting someone or had suddenly seen a person with whom she wished to speak in private.

The trees were dripping with rain. The air smelled strongly of damp earth. Cows stared at the car, chewing their cud . . .

The mayor peered all around, perhaps expecting to spot his wife behind a hedge or tree trunk.

'Look closely!' said Maigret, as if training a rookie.

There were some recognizable tracks on the road to Dives. A vehicle had stopped there, had some trouble turning around on the narrow road and driven off again.

'An old van. Let's go, driver!'

They did not drive far. Well before Dives, the tracks vanished near a stony side road. Monsieur Grandmaison was still tense, his eyes glittering with both anxiety and hatred.

'What do you think?'

'There's a small village that way, about five hundred metres on.'

'In which case, we'd best leave the car here.'

Exhaustion gave Maigret a look of inhuman indifference. He was literally asleep on his feet. He seemed to advance thanks only to his own momentum. Anyone watching them walk along that road would have thought the mayor was in charge, and the inspector, some underling following placidly in his wake.

They passed a little house surrounded by chickens, where a woman stared at the two men in amazement. Then they arrived at the back of a church not much bigger than a thatched cottage and, to the left, a tobacconist's shop.

'You don't mind?' asked Maigret, bringing out his empty pouch.

He stepped inside the little shop, which sold groceries and all sorts of household items. An elderly man emerged from a room with a vaulted ceiling and summoned his daughter to bring Maigret his tobacco. While the door was open, the inspector glimpsed a wall telephone.

'At what time did my friend come here to place a call this morning?'

'A good hour ago,' replied the girl promptly.

'So the lady has arrived?'

'Oh, yes. She even came in here for directions. They're not complicated, it's the last house, the lane on the right.'

Maigret left, still moving like a sleepwalker. He found Monsieur Grandmaison standing in front of the church, looking all around in a manner certain to arouse the suspicions of the entire village.

'It occurs to me,' murmured Maigret, 'that we should split up. You search off to the left, by the fields, while I look on the right.'

He caught a gleam of delight in the man's eye. The mayor could not hide his hope of finding his wife on his own and talking privately with her.

'Good idea,' he replied, feigning indifference.

The hamlet consisted of no more than twenty poky little houses that clumped together enough in one area to give the illusion of a street, which did not prevent real manure from piling up there. It was still raining, a rain so fine it was almost a mist, and no one was outdoors. Curtains were twitching, however. One could just imagine, behind them, the usual wrinkled old women peering out from their dimly lit homes.

At the very end of the hamlet, in front of the fenced-in meadow where two horses were galloping around, there was a single-storey building with a crooked roof and two front steps. Maigret looked back, heard the mayor's footsteps at the other end of the village, then walked into the house without knocking.

Something moved in the shadows that pressed in on the

glowing hearth. A black shape; the white patch of an old woman's house cap.

She hobbled over, bent almost in two.

'What d'you want?'

The stuffy room smelled of straw, cabbage and chicken coops. There were even chicks pecking around by the fireplace.

Maigret's head almost touched the ceiling. Noticing a door at the far end of the room, he realized that speed was in order. Without a word, he marched over and opened the door: Madame Grandmaison was busy writing, with Jean Martineau standing next to her.

There was a moment of surprise and dismay. The woman rose from her straw-bottomed chair. Martineau's first impulse was to grab and crumple up her piece of paper. Both of them instinctively drew close together.

The cottage had only these two rooms, and this was the old woman's bedroom. On the whitewashed walls, two portraits and some cheap chromos in black-and-gold frames. A very high bed. The table where Madame Grandmaison had been writing was the wash stand, from which the basin had been set aside.

'Your husband will be here in a few minutes!' announced Maigret, by way of an introduction.

'Is that your doing?' demanded Martineau angrily.

'Hush, Raymond.'

She had used his first name – and called him not Jean, but Raymond. Reflecting on these details, Maigret went to listen briefly at the front door.

'Will you give me the letter you were writing?'

The couple looked at each other. Madame Grandmaison

was pale and wan. Maigret had seen her once before, but only in the performance of her most sacred duties as a woman of her social standing: receiving guests at home.

At that time he had been impressed by her perfect performance and the conventional graciousness with which she could offer a cup of tea or respond to a compliment.

He had imagined her life: the cares of a household in Caen, the social occasions, the children's upbringing. Two or three months spent at health spas or luxury resorts. A certain level of vanity, but more concern about her dignity than her beauty.

Something of all that doubtless remained in the woman now before him, but there was a new element. She was in fact showing more sang-froid, even more raw nerve than her companion, who seemed on the verge of real collapse.

'Give him the paper,' she said, as Martineau was about to tear it up.

There was almost nothing on it.

Dear Headmaster,
    Would you be kind enough to . . .

The large, backwards-sloping hand of every girl educated at boarding school at the turn of the century.

'You received two telephone calls this morning, didn't you? One from your husband . . . Or rather, you were the one who called, to tell him you would be arriving in Ouistreham. Then a call from Monsieur Martineau, asking you to come here. He had you picked up at the crossroads by a small van.'

Just then Maigret saw something he hadn't noticed

before, on the table, behind the ink pot: a neat pile of thousand-franc bills.

Martineau followed his eyes . . . Too late to do anything! And too much for him: he collapsed in sudden lethargy on the edge of the old woman's bed and stared despondently at the floor.

'Are you the one who brought him that money?'

And once again, there was the same feeling that had marked this entire case. The same atmosphere as when Maigret had caught Big Louis beating the mayor in his villa in Ouistreham – and both men had refused to talk! The same atmosphere as when the crew of the *Saint-Michel* had refused to answer him the night before!

A fierce refusal, an absolute determination not to explain anything at all.

'I suppose this letter is addressed to the headmaster of a boarding school. Your son is at Stanislas, so the letter probably concerns him. As for the money . . . Of course! Martineau must have abandoned the grounded schooner to swim to shore, and in his hurry he probably left his wallet behind. You brought him some money so that—'

Maigret abruptly changed the subject, and his tone:

'And the others, Martineau? All safe and sound?'

The man hesitated, but could not keep himself, in the end, from blinking in affirmation.

'I won't ask you where they're hiding. I know you won't tell.'

'True!'

'*What's true?*'

Someone had just pushed the front door wide open. The outraged voice was the mayor's – and he was unrecognizable.

Panting with anger, fists clenched, tensed to spring at the enemy, he glared at his wife, at Martineau, at the money still lying on the table.

But the menace in his eyes betrayed fear, too, and the dread of disaster.

'What's true? What did he say? What new lies is he telling? . . . And her? She's the one . . .'

Choking, he couldn't get the words out. Maigret watched, prepared to intervene.

'What's true? What's going on! . . . Are they plotting something? . . . And whose money is that?'

The old woman was bustling about in the front room, calling her chickens to the door.

'Here, chick-chick! Chick-chick!'

The scattered corn clattered softly down on the blue-stone steps. A neighbour's hen was fended off with a foot.

'G'won home with you, Blackie . . .'

In the bedroom, nothing. Heavy silence. As pallid and depressing as the sky that rainy morning.

People possessed by fear. Because they were afraid! All of them! Martineau, the woman, the mayor . . . It was as if each one of them were alone with that fear . . . Each one afraid in a different way!

Then Maigret spoke slowly and solemnly, like a judge.

'I have been instructed by the public prosecutor to find and arrest the murderer of Captain Joris, wounded by a bullet to the head and, six weeks later, poisoned in his bed with strychnine. Does anyone here wish to make a statement regarding this crime?'

Until that moment, no one had noticed that the room

was unheated. Yet suddenly, they felt cold . . . Each syllable had rung out as if in a church. The words still seemed to linger in the air. *Poisoned . . . Strychnine . . .*

Especially Maigret's last question.

Does anyone here wish to make a statement? . . .

Martineau was the first to hang his head. Madame Grandmaison, her eyes gleaming, kept looking back and forth between him and her husband.

But no one said a thing. No one dared face the look in Maigret's eyes, which seemed to grow darker.

Two minutes . . . Three minutes . . . The old woman put a few logs on the fire in the next room.

Then Maigret's voice, again, deliberately curt and stripped of all emotion.

'In the name of the law, Jean Martineau, I arrest you.'

A woman's scream. Madame Grandmaison flung herself desperately at Martineau but fell in a faint almost at the same instant.

With a savage look, the mayor turned towards the wall.

And Martineau heaved a sigh of weary resignation, not daring even to go to help the unconscious woman.

It was Maigret who bent down to her, then looked around for the water jug from the wash stand.

He went to ask the old woman for some vinegar, the smell of which now mingled with the already complex odour of the cottage.

A few moments later Madame Grandmaison came to, and, after a few uncontrollable sobs, sank into an almost complete state of prostration.

'Do you think you can walk?'

She nodded. She could walk, but in a jolting, uneven way.

'You will follow me, gentlemen, will you not? I trust that I may count, *this time*, on your compliance?'

The old woman watched them cross her kitchen in some consternation. Only after they were outside did she rush to the door.

'You're coming back for lunch, then, Monsieur Raymond?'

Raymond! It was the second time he had been called that. The man shook his head.

The four of them walked on through the village. Martineau stopped in front of the little shop, hesitated, and turned to Maigret.

'Please forgive me, but as I'm not sure I'll ever return here, I don't wish to leave any unpaid debts behind. I owe these people for a phone call, a grog and a pack of cigarettes.'

It was Maigret who paid. They walked around the church and at the end of the stony road found the car waiting for them. After telling them all to get in, the inspector paused to think before speaking to the driver.

'To Ouistreham. There you will stop first at the police station.'

The journey took place in complete silence. Rain still fell from a sky of solid grey as a freshening wind shook the dripping trees.

Outside the police station, Maigret had Martineau get out and gave instructions to Lucas.

'Keep him in the lock-up. You're responsible for him! Anything new here?'

'The tug's arrived. They're waiting for the tide to come in.'

The car drove away. When they swung by the harbour, Maigret made another short stop.

It was noon. The lock workers were at their posts, because a steamer was due in from Caen. The strip of sand along the beach had narrowed and the foaming waves were almost licking at the dunes.

On the right, a crowd watched a fascinating spectacle: the tug from Trouville was anchored not 500 metres off the coast. A dinghy was fighting its way over to the *Saint-Michel*, now half righted with the incoming tide.

Maigret noticed that the mayor was also watching the drama, from inside the car. Then Captain Delcourt came out of the bar.

'Will it work?' asked Maigret.

'I think we'll save her. For the last two hours we've been lightening her, removing ballast. If we can keep her from breaking adrift . . .'

And he looked up at the sky as if reading the vagaries of the wind on a map.

'It's just that we have to finish before the tide turns again.'

Glimpsing the mayor and his wife inside their car, he nodded to them deferentially, then gave Maigret a questioning look.

'Anything new?'

'Don't know.'

Lucas was approaching, and he did have news, but he drew his chief aside before delivering it.

'We've got Big Louis.'

'What?'

'He slipped up! This morning the police in Dives found tracks through some fields. The footsteps of a man walking straight ahead and clambering over the hedgerows. The trail led to the Orne, to the place where a fisherman kept his rowing boat hauled up on the bank. Except that the boat was on the other side of the river.'

'The officers followed him?'

'Yes, and came to the beach, more or less opposite the *Saint-Michel*. At the edge of the dunes over there is a—'

'Ruined chapel!'

'You already know?'

'Notre-Dame-des-Dunes.'

'Right. They nabbed Big Louis there. He was holed up, watching the salvage operation. When I arrived he was begging the officers not to take him away yet, so that he could watch from the beach until the job was done. I gave permission. He's still there, in handcuffs. And shouting instructions! He's afraid they'll lose his boat . . . Don't you want to see him?'

'I don't know . . . maybe, in a little while.'

For the Grandmaisons were still waiting in the car.

'You think we'll ever get to the bottom of this?'

No reply.

'Personally,' continued Lucas, 'I'm beginning to think we won't. They're all liars! And the ones who aren't lying won't talk, even though they know something! It's as if everyone around here were responsible for Joris' death . . .'

But the inspector simply shrugged and walked away muttering, 'See you later . . .'

Back in the car, he surprised the chauffeur by telling him, 'Back to the house, now,' as if he were speaking of his own home.

'The house in Caen?'

To tell the truth, the inspector hadn't meant that, but the chauffeur had given him an idea.

'Yes, in Caen!'

Monsieur Grandmaison scowled. His wife, though, could not react at all. She seemed to be allowing events to carry her along and offered not the slightest resistance.

Between the city gates and Rue du Four, a good fifty hats were doffed. Everyone appeared to recognize Monsieur Grandmaison's car. And the greetings were respectful. The ship-owner was like a nobleman travelling through his domain.

'A simple formality,' said Maigret casually when they arrived at the house. 'Please excuse me for having brought you here, but as I mentioned this morning, this affair must be resolved by tonight.'

A calm street, lined with imposing mansions of a kind found only in the provinces these days. The house, its stones dark with age, was fronted by a courtyard. And on the gate was a brass plaque with the name of the family's shipping company.

Inside the courtyard, a sign with an arrow: 'Office'.

Another sign, another arrow: 'Cashier's Office'.

And one last notice. 'Office Hours: 9 a.m. to 4 p.m.'

It was shortly past noon. The drive from Ouistreham had taken only ten minutes. Most of the firm's employees had already left for lunch by then, but a few were still at their desks, in dark, solemn offices with thick carpets and heavy Louis-Philippe furniture.

'I will probably ask you later on to spare me a few moments of your time, madame, but for the moment, would you like to retire to your rooms?'

The entire ground floor was given over to offices. The vestibule was spacious, flanked with large cast-iron candelabra. A marble staircase led up to the first floor, where the family lived.

The mayor of Ouistreham was waiting gloomily for Maigret to deal with him.

'What is it you want from me?' he asked quietly.

He turned up his collar and jammed his hat down to keep his staff from seeing what Big Louis' fists had done to him.

'Nothing in particular. Simply permission to come and go, to get the feel of the house.'

'Do you need me for anything?'

'Not at all.'

'In that case, if I may, I will go and join Madame Grand-maison.'

His respectful reference to his wife was in sharp contrast with that morning's events in the old woman's cottage. After watching him vanish upstairs, Maigret went to the far end of the vestibule to make sure the building had only one exit.

Leaving the mansion, he found a local policeman and stationed him near the front gate.

'Got it? Let everyone leave, except Monsieur Grand-maison. Will you recognize him?'

'Well, of course! But, what's he done? A fine man like him
. . . He's president of the chamber of commerce, you know!'

'So much the better!'

In the vestibule, an office on the right: 'Secretary'. Maigret
knocked, pushed open the door, smelled a whiff of cigar,
but saw no one.

The office on the left: 'Director'.

Again, the same resolutely solemn atmosphere, the
same dark-red carpets, the gilt wallpaper, the elaborate
ceiling mouldings.

The impression that within these walls, no one would dare
to raise his voice. Dignified gentlemen in morning coats and
striped trousers would smoke fat cigars and pontificate.

A solid business indeed! A well-established provincial
firm, handed down from father to son for generations.

'Monsieur Grandmaison? His signature is as good as gold.'

And here was Maigret in his office, which was furnished
in the opulent Empire style, more suitable for an important
businessman. On the walls, statistical tables, graphs,
colour-coded schedules, photographs of ships.

As he was walking around, his hands in his pockets, a
door opened, and a rather anxious, white-haired old man
popped his head in.

'What's the . . .'

'Police!' replied Maigret sharply, as if savouring the
explosive effect of his words in that place.

And the old fellow went into a terrified dither.

'Don't worry, monsieur. Your employer has asked me
to look into a few things. And you are . . .'

'The head cashier,' replied the man hastily.

'Then you would be the man who's been with the firm for . . . for . . .'

'Forty-two years. I began here in Monsieur Charles' time.'

'Right. And that's your office, next door? In short, you're now the one who runs everything, aren't you? At least that's what I hear . . .'

Maigret was sitting pretty. He had seen the house, and one look at this old man was all he needed.

'It's only natural, isn't it! When Monsieur Ernest is not here . . .'

'Monsieur Ernest?'

'Yes, well, Monsieur Grandmaison! I've known him since he was a boy, so I still call him Monsieur Ernest.'

Maigret had eased himself into the old man's office, a place devoid of luxury and apparently not open to outsiders. And here files and documents were piled up in profusion.

On a cluttered table, some sandwiches sitting on their butcher's paper. On the stove, a small steaming coffee pot.

'You even eat here, monsieur . . . Forgive me, I've gone and forgotten your name.'

'Bernardin. But everyone here calls me Old Bernard. As I live alone, there's no point in me going home for lunch like the others. In fact, is it about that small theft last week that Monsieur Ernest has called you in? . . . He should have spoken to me, because it's all sorted out now. A young man who'd taken two thousand francs, and his uncle has paid us back. The young man swore . . . Well, you know, at that age! . . . He'd fallen into some bad company.'

'We'll see about that presently. But do go on with your lunch . . . So, you were already Monsieur Charles' trusted lieutenant before being his son's.'

'I was the cashier. Back then there was no chief cashier – and I might even say that the position was created just for me!'

'Monsieur Ernest was an only son?'

'Yes. There was a daughter, married off to a businessman in Lille, but she died in childbirth along with her infant.'

'But what of Monsieur Raymond?'

The old man's head jerked up in surprise.

'Ah! Monsieur Ernest has told you?'

Old Bernard now seemed more on his guard.

'Wasn't he part of the family?'

'A cousin. A Grandmaison, but a poor relation. His father died out in the colonies. It happens in every family, doesn't it . . .'

'Indeed it does!' Maigret agreed readily.

'Monsieur Ernest's father more or less adopted him . . . That is, he found a place for him here . . .'

Maigret needed more information and dropped all pretence.

'One moment, Monsieur Bernard! I'd like to make sure I've got everything straight. The founder of the Anglo-Normande was Monsieur Charles Grandmaison, correct? Monsieur Charles Grandmaison had an only son, Monsieur Ernest, currently in charge.'

'Yes.'

The inspector's inquisitorial tone puzzled the old man, who was beginning to get worried.

'Good! Monsieur Charles had a brother who died in the colonies and who also had a son, Monsieur Raymond Grandmaison.'

'Yes, but I—'

'Just a moment! And go on with your lunch, please. This Monsieur Raymond, a penniless orphan, was taken in here by his uncle. A position was found for him in the firm. Which one, exactly?'

'Well,' replied the old man hesitantly, 'he was assigned to the freight department. As a kind of office manager.'

'Fine. Monsieur Charles Grandmaison died. Monsieur Ernest took over. Monsieur Raymond was still here.'

'Yes.'

'They quarrelled. One moment! Was Monsieur Ernest already married at the time?'

'I'm not sure that I should say anything.'

'I advise you strongly to cooperate if you don't want to have problems with the law, elderly though you may be.'

'The law! Has Monsieur Raymond returned?'

'Never mind that. Was Monsieur Ernest married?'

'No. Not yet.'

'Right. Monsieur Ernest was the boss. His cousin, Raymond, still an office manager. What happened?'

'I'm not sure I have the right . . .'

'I give you the right.'

'It's like this in every family. Monsieur Ernest was a responsible, reliable man, like his father. Even at the age when boys naturally rebel against authority, he was already as serious as he is now.'

'And Monsieur Raymond?'

'Quite the opposite!'

'And?'

'I'm the only one here who knows, aside from Monsieur Ernest. Some irregularities were discovered in the accounts . . . Involving large sums . . .'

'So?'

'Monsieur Raymond disappeared. That's to say, instead of having him arrested, Monsieur Ernest strongly advised him to go and live abroad.'

'In Norway?'

'I don't know. I never heard his name mentioned again.'

'Monsieur Ernest was married soon after that?'

'That's right. A few months later.'

The walls were lined with filing cabinets of a doleful green. The faithful old man was eating without any appetite, still worried, feeling guilty for letting the inspector worm information out of him.

'And how long ago was that?'

'Let me see . . . It was the year they widened the canal. Fifteen years ago, or just about.'

Footsteps had been going back and forth in the room above their heads for a few minutes now.

'The dining room?' asked Maigret.

'Yes.'

And then the footsteps overhead went faster . . . A dull thud – as a body fell to the floor.

Old Bernard was whiter than the butcher's paper on his desk.

13. The House Across the Street

Monsieur Grandmaison was dead. Lying across the carpet, his head near a table leg, his feet over by the window, he seemed enormous. Very little blood. The bullet had entered between two ribs and lodged in his heart.

As for the revolver, it lay next to his lifeless hand.

Madame Grandmaison was not weeping. She stood leaning against the monumental mantelpiece, staring at her husband as if she had not yet grasped what had happened.

'It's over,' said Maigret simply, and got to his feet.

A large room, sad and severe. Dark curtains at windows that let in a bleak light.

'Did he say anything to you?'

She shook her head, then made an effort to speak.

'Ever since we got home,' she stammered, 'he'd been pacing up and down. Several times he turned to me, and I thought he was going to tell me something . . . Then suddenly, the shot came – and I hadn't even seen the gun!'

She spoke as women do when they are profoundly shaken and struggling to make sense of their own thoughts, but her eyes were dry.

It was clear that she had never loved Grandmaison, at least not passionately. He was her husband. She was a dutiful wife. A kind of affection had sprung up as they'd grown used to living together.

But before his dead body, she displayed none of those wrenching emotions that betoken real love.

Instead, dazed and exhausted, she asked, 'Was it him?'

'It was.'

Then there was silence around the immense body bathed in harsh daylight. The inspector watched Madame Grandmaison. He saw her look out at the street, searching for something across the way, and a feeling of nostalgia seemed to soften her features.

'Would you allow me to ask you two or three questions before the others arrive?'

She nodded.

'Did you know Raymond before you met your husband?'

'I lived across the street.'

A grey house much like the one they were in. Above the front door, the brass plate of a notary.

'I loved Raymond. He loved me. His cousin was courting me as well, but in his own way.'

'Two quite different men, weren't they?'

'Ernest was already as you knew him. A cold man, who seemed never to have been young. Raymond, well, he had a bad reputation because his life was too big and wild to fit into the small-town mould. That and his lack of fortune were why my father did not want me to marry him.'

It was eerie, listening to these personal confessions murmured next to a corpse. They were like the dismal summing-up of a whole life.

'Were you Raymond's mistress?'

She blinked in affirmation.

'And he left?'

'Without telling a soul. One night. I learned about it from his cousin. Left with some of the company money.'

'And Ernest married you. Your son is not his, I take it?'

'He is Raymond's son. You see, when he left and I was on my own, I knew I was going to have a child. And Ernest was asking me to marry him. Look at these two houses, this street, this city where everyone knows everyone else.'

'You told Ernest the truth?'

'Yes. He married me anyway. The child was born in Italy; I stayed there for more than a year to avoid nasty gossip. I thought my husband had been a kind of hero . . .'

'And?'

She turned away: she had just caught sight of the body again.

'I don't know,' she sighed. 'I believe that he did love me,' she continued reluctantly, 'but after his own fashion. He wanted me. He got me. Can you understand? A man incapable of impulse, of spirit. Once married, he lived as before: for himself. I was part of his household. Somewhat like a trusted employee. I don't know if he received any news of Raymond later on, but when the boy came across a picture of him one day and asked Ernest about him, he simply said, "A cousin who turned out badly."'

Maigret seemed gripped by some profound concern, for it was a whole way of life he was attempting to piece together. More than that, it was the life of a family business, of the very family itself!

That life had lasted fifteen years! New steamships had been bought. There had been receptions in this very room, bridge parties and afternoon teas. There had been baptisms.

Summers at Ouistreham and in the mountains.

And now, Madame Grandmaison was so weary that she collapsed into an armchair, passing a limp hand over her face.

'I don't understand,' she stammered. 'This captain whom I never saw . . . You really think . . . ?'

Maigret turned away to listen, then went to open the door. The old man was on the landing, fearful but too deferential to enter the room. He looked searchingly at the inspector.

'Monsieur Grandmaison is dead. Call the family doctor. Do not announce the news to the employees and servants until later.'

He closed the door, almost took his pipe from his pocket and shrugged.

To his surprise, he felt growing respect and sympathy for this woman, who had struck him, the first time he had seen her, as an ordinary 'lady of the house'.

'Was it your husband, yesterday, who sent you to Paris?'

'Yes. I hadn't known that Raymond was in France. My husband simply asked me to get my son at Stanislas and spend a few days with him in the South of France. Although I thought this somewhat peculiar, I did as he asked, but when I arrived at the Hôtel de Lutèce, Ernest telephoned to ask me to return home without going on to the boarding school.'

'And this morning, Raymond called you here?'

'Yes, with an urgent request. He begged me to bring him a little money. He swore that our lives – all our lives – would otherwise be torn apart.'

'He did not accuse your husband of anything?'

'No. Back there, in the cottage, he never even mentioned him, but spoke of friends, a few seamen to whom he had to give some money so that they could leave the country. He spoke of some kind of shipwreck.'

The doctor arrived, a friend of the family who stared at the corpse in consternation.

'Monsieur Grandmaison has killed himself!' announced Maigret firmly. 'It is for you to discover what illness has carried him off. You understand me? And I will deal with the police . . .'

He went to take leave of Madame Grandmaison, who finally summoned the courage to say, 'You have not told me why . . .'

'Raymond will tell you one day. Ah, one last question. On the 16th of September, your son was in Ouistreham with your husband, was he not?'

'Yes. He stayed there until the 20th . . .'

Maigret bowed himself out, tramped downstairs and walked through the offices with drooping shoulders and a heavy heart.

Outdoors, he breathed more deeply and stood bareheaded in the rain, as if to refresh himself, to dispel the oppressive atmosphere of that house.

Turning, he took one last look up at the windows. Another at those across the street, where Madame Grandmaison had spent her youth.

A sigh.

'Come on!'

Maigret stood in the open door to the empty room

where Raymond had been kept. He beckoned to him to follow, then led him out to the street and the road to the harbour.

Raymond was surprised and somewhat worried by this unexpected release.

'Haven't you anything to tell me?' grumbled Maigret with a show of irritation.

'No!'

'You won't defend yourself against the charges?'

'I'll keep telling the court that I haven't killed anyone!'

'But you won't tell the truth?'

Raymond hung his head.

They were beginning to catch glimpses of the sea and could hear the tug whistling as it moved towards the jetties, towing the *Saint-Michel* at the end of a steel cable.

It was then that Maigret announced impassively, as if it were the most natural thing in the world: 'Grandmaison is dead.'

'What? . . . What did you say?'

Raymond caught Maigret's arm in a fierce grip.

'He's . . . ?'

'He killed himself an hour ago, in his house.'

'Did he say anything?'

'No. He paced up and down his dining room for a quarter of an hour and then shot himself. That's it!'

They kept walking. In the distance they could see the excited crowd on the jetties, watching the salvage operation.

'So now you can tell me the truth, Raymond Grandmaison. Besides, I already know the gist of it. You were trying to get your son back, weren't you!'

No reply.

'You had help from Captain Joris, among others. And unfortunately for him, as it turned out.'

'Don't say it! If you only knew . . .'

'Come this way, there will be fewer people.'

The narrow path led down to a deserted beach pounded by waves.

'Did you really take off with some of the company funds?'

'Is that what Hélène told you?' Now his voice was bitter. 'Yes . . . Ernest must have told her his own version of what happened . . . I'm not claiming to have been a saint, far from it! I was looking for a good time, as they say. And above all, at least for a while, I was enthralled by gambling. I won, I lost. Then came the day when, yes, I helped myself to some company money. My cousin found out.

'I promised to pay it back over time and pleaded with him to keep the whole thing quiet. He really did want to call in the police but agreed not to, on one condition: that I leave the country and never set foot in France again! You understand? He wanted Hélène . . . and he got her.'

Smiling sadly, Raymond was quiet for a few moments.

'Others head down south or out east, but I went north and set myself up in Norway. I never heard any news from home . . . The letters I wrote to Hélène went unanswered, and yesterday I learned that she'd never received them.

'I wrote to my cousin, too, with no more success.

'I won't pretend to be better than I am or try to make you feel sorry for me with a tale of unhappy love. No . . . In the beginning I didn't think much about it. There, you can see

I'm being sincere! I was working, having all sorts of problems . . . But at night, I felt a kind of dull, aching nostalgia.

'There were disappointments . . . I started a business; it ended badly. For years I went through ups and downs in a country where I was an outsider.

'I'd changed my name there. To try tipping the scales in my favour as a businessman, I became a naturalized citizen as well.

'Now and then I'd entertain officers from some French ship, and that's how I discovered one day that I had a son.

'I wasn't sure! But when I thought about the dates . . . I couldn't stop thinking about it and wrote to Ernest. I begged him to tell me the truth, to let me come home to France, if only for a few days.

'He sent me a telegram: "Arrest at French border".

'Years went by; I was bent on making money. There's not much to say about that, except that there was a hollow place in my heart.

'In Tromsø there are three months of endless night every year. Regrets and longings grow sharper . . . Sometimes I would have attacks of hysterical rage.

'I set myself a goal: to become as rich as my cousin. And I did! Thanks to the cod roe business. But it was when I achieved this success that I felt the most miserable.

'Then suddenly, I came back here. I was determined to act. Yes! After fifteen years! I was looking around Ouistreham and . . . I saw my boy, on the beach. I saw Hélène, at a distance . . .

'And I wondered how I had ever managed to live without my son. Do you understand me?

'I bought a boat. If I had acted openly, my cousin would

not have hesitated for a moment to have me arrested. Because he had kept all the evidence he needed!

'You saw the men helping me: good men, no matter what they look like. Everything was arranged.

'Ernest Grandmaison and the boy were alone in the house that night. To be even more certain of success, to increase the odds in my favour, I'd asked Captain Joris to help. I'd met him in Norway, when he was still going to sea. He knew the mayor and was to visit him under some pretext and distract him while Big Louis and I were spiriting my son away.

'And that – *that* was what caused the tragedy. While Joris was with my cousin in the study, Big Louis and I had come in through the back door, but unfortunately, we knocked over a broom in the corridor.

'Grandmaison heard the noise, thought someone was after him and got his revolver from the desk drawer.

'What happened next . . . I truly don't know, there was such confusion! Joris followed Grandmaison out to the corridor, which was completely dark. A shot – and of all the bad luck, Joris was hit!

'I was beside myself with anguish. I didn't want any scandal, especially for Hélène's sake. How could I have told that whole story to the police!

'Big Louis and I carried Joris aboard the *Saint-Michel*. He needed medical attention, so we headed for England and arrived there a few hours later. But we couldn't go ashore without passports! There were police officers and watchmen on the quay.

'I'd studied a little medicine once upon a time and did my best for Joris on the ship, but it was nowhere near enough. We set out for Holland. That's where the surgeons cleaned up the wound. The clinic could not keep him there, however, without informing the authorities.

'We sailed on, a ghastly voyage! Can you imagine us all on the ship, and Joris at death's door? He needed weeks of rest and care. I almost took him to Norway on the *Saint-Michel*, but then we encountered a schooner bound for the Lofoten islands. I moved Joris with me to that schooner; we were safer at sea than on land.

'He stayed a week at home with me in Tromsø. Again, though, people began to wonder who my mysterious guest was, and we had to set out again. Copenhagen, Hamburg . . . Joris was getting better; the wound had scarred over, but he'd lost his reason and was unable to speak.

'What could I do with him, I ask you? And wouldn't he stand a better chance of recovering his reason in his own home, in familiar surroundings, instead of while running from pillar to post?

'I wanted at least to secure his material comfort. I sent three hundred thousand francs to his bank, signing his name for deposit to his account.

'I still had to get him home! It was too risky for me to bring him here to Ouistreham myself. Releasing him in Paris . . . Would that not bring him inevitably to the attention of the police, who would identify him and send him home?

'And that's what happened. There was only one thing I couldn't have anticipated: that my cousin, terrified that Joris might one day reveal who'd shot him, would do away with the captain in that cowardly way.

'Because he is the one who put the strychnine in the

water carafe. He simply went in the cottage through the back door when he was going off duck hunting.'

'And you got back to work,' said Maigret slowly.

'What else could I do! I wanted my son! But now my cousin was on his guard. The boy was back at Stanislas, beyond my reach.'

Maigret knew about that part. And now, looking around at the setting he had come to know so well, he understood more clearly what was at stake in the secret battle between the two men.

And not just between the two of them! A struggle against *him*, Maigret!

The police had to be kept in the dark, for neither one of the cousins could afford to tell the truth.

'I came here on the *Saint-Michel* . . .'

'I know! And you sent Big Louis to the mayor's house.'

Raymond couldn't help smiling as the inspector went on.

'A Big Louis primed for battle, who took revenge on Grandmaison for all the powerful men who'd persecuted him! He could pound him to his heart's content, knowing that his victim would never let out a peep to the police. He must have forced him to write a letter authorizing you to take the boy out of school.'

'Yes. I was behind the villa with your colleague on my heels. Big Louis left the letter in a pre-arranged spot, and I shook off your man. I took a bicycle; I bought a car in Caen. I had to move fast. While I was getting my son, Big Louis stayed with the mayor to keep him from alerting the school. A waste of time, as it turned out, since he'd already sent Hélène to pick up the boy ahead of me.

'Then you had me arrested.

'It was all over . . . I couldn't go after her while you were stubbornly digging up the truth.

'Our only recourse was to escape. If we stayed, you would inevitably work everything out.

'And that explains last night. Bad luck just wouldn't let us go . . . The schooner grounded on the shoal, and we had a hard time of it, swimming ashore. To cap it all, I lost my wallet.

'No money! The police on our track . . . All I could do was call Hélène to ask her for a few thousand francs, enough to get the four of us to the border . . . In Norway, I could pay my companions what I owed them. And Hélène came at once.

'But so did you! You, whom we constantly found blocking our way. You, relentless, to whom we could say nothing, whom I could hardly warn that you might provoke more harm through your inquiry!'

His eyes now betrayed a sudden misgiving, and in a faltering voice he asked:

'Did my cousin *really* kill himself?'

Had Maigret lied to him, perhaps, to induce him to speak?

'Yes, he did kill himself, when he realized that the truth would come out in the end. And he understood *that* when I arrested you. He guessed that I'd done that simply to give him time to think things over.'

The two men had been walking as they talked; now they stopped abruptly together on the jetty. The *Saint-Michel* was going slowly past, with an old fisherman proudly at the wheel.

Someone ran up, pushing his way roughly through the

gawking crowd, the first man to leap on to the schooner's deck.

Big Louis!

He had given his captors the slip, snapped the chain between his handcuffs! Hustling the fisherman aside, he grabbed the wheel.

'Slow down, for God's sake!' he yelled to the men aboard the tug. 'You'll bash her up!'

'And the other two?' Maigret asked Raymond.

'This morning you passed within a metre of them. They're hiding out in the village, in the old woman's woodshed.'

Lucas was making his way through the crowd towards Maigret, looking surprised.

'Listen, we've got them!'

'Who?'

'Lannec and Célestin . . .'

'They're here?'

'The Dives police have just brought them in.'

'Well, tell them to let those two go. And have them both come to the harbour.'

They stood facing Captain Joris' cottage and his garden, its last roses stripped of their petals by the storm. Behind a curtain, someone looking out: it was Julie, wondering if the man at the wheel on the schooner was really her brother. Near Captain Delcourt, the lock workers and harbour men stood together, watching.

'Those fellows . . . The trouble they caused me, with their half-truths and evasions!' sighed Maigret.

Raymond smiled.

'They're sailors!'

'I know! And sailors don't like a landlubber like me sticking my nose into their business.'

He filled his pipe with little taps of his index finger. Puffing gently on the fresh pipe, he frowned.

'What will we tell them?'

Ernest Grandmaison was dead. Must they reveal that he was a murderer?

'Perhaps we could . . .' Raymond began.

'I don't know . . . Claim that it was some old feud? A vengeful sailor, a foreigner, who's gone back to his country . . .'

The crew of the tug was tramping off to the Buvette de la Marine, beckoning the lock workers to join them.

And Big Louis was bustling about his boat, patting and touching it as if he were checking a lost dog come home, making sure she wasn't hurt.

'Hey there!' Maigret called to him.

Big Louis gave a start but hesitated to step forwards – or more likely, to leave his schooner again. When he noticed Raymond standing there too, he seemed as surprised as Lucas had been.

'What the . . . ?'

'When can the *Saint-Michel* go back to sea?' asked Maigret.

'Right away if need be! No damage anywhere! She's a trim little ship, I promise you.'

Big Louis was looking questioningly at Raymond, who announced, 'In that case, take off on a sail-about with Lannec and Célestin . . .'

'They're here too?'

'They're coming . . . Go on a sailing spree for a few

weeks. And far enough away that they forget about the *Saint-Michel* around here.'

'Well, I might take my sister along as ship's cook . . . She's fearless, you know, our Julie.'

Still, he was a bit hangdog around Maigret. He hadn't forgotten the ship's run for it the night before and had no idea if he could treat it lightly.

'You weren't too cold, at least, were you?' he asked the inspector.

Big Louis was now standing at the edge of the dock, off which Maigret sent him splashing with one push.

'I believe I've got a train at six o'clock,' he observed pleasantly.

Still, he made no move to leave. He looked around him with a pang of nostalgia, as if he had already grown fond of the little harbour town.

Didn't he know it in all its nooks and crannies, in all its moods, in shivery morning sunshine and blustery tempest, fogbound or streaming with rain?

'Will you be going to Caen?' he asked Raymond, who was sticking close to his side.

'Not right away. I think it would be better . . . to let . . .'

'Some time pass . . . Yes.'

When Lucas returned fifteen minutes later and asked after Maigret, he was waved over to the Buvette de la Marine, which had just lit its lamps.

He could see the inspector through the misted-over windows. An inspector solidly straddling a cane-seated chair, pipe clenched in his teeth, a glass of beer within reach, listening to the stories being told around him by men in rubber boots and sailor caps.

And on the ten o'clock train that evening, that same inspector sighed, 'They must be snug and warm in the cabin, all three of them . . .'

'What cabin?'

'Aboard the *Saint-Michel*! With the gimballed lamp, the nicked-up table, those thick glasses and that bottle of Dutch gin . . . And the purring stove . . . Say, have you got a match?'